BOMBSHELL

NEW YORK TIMES BESTSELLING AUTHOR

ABBI
GLINES

JUDGEMENT SERIES
BOOK ONE

Bombshell

Good Girl
Carrie Underwood

Good Girls Bad Guys
Falling in Reverse

Bad Boys
Zara Larsson

Good Girls Go Bad
Cobra Starship and Leighton Meester

Criminal
Britney Spears

I'd Lie
Taylor Swift

Playlist

Kiss Me Slowly
Parachute

Better Man
Paolo Nutini

If I didn't Love You
Jason Aldean and Carrie Underwood

In Case You Didn't Know
Brett Young

You are the Reason
Calum Scott and Leona Lewis

To every good girl who has loved a bad boy.

1

"*You only deserve what you make yourself worthy of.*"
—*Abbi Glines*

Prologue

DOLLY BELLE DIXON

Twelve Years Ago

*I*t had been two days, and Momma hadn't come out of her bedroom. Once the church folks and neighbors stopped coming by with casseroles, cakes, pies, and their condolences, she'd shut herself off in her room. The only sound I heard from her was the crying. Her door was locked, and I couldn't get her to answer me when I knocked.

I sat outside her room in the hallway. My arms wrapped around my knees as I rocked back and forth. "One hundred twenty-two, one hundred twenty-two, one hundred twenty-two." I whispered the number over and over again, trying to block out the sounds of her sobbing.

My own eyes burned with unshed tears, and I feared the lump in my throat had become permanent. It had been there since the moment I'd found Daddy. It had thickened as I made the way from the garage, where he hung—his neck bent at an odd angle, face blue, and body limp—to find my mother in the kitchen.

"One hundred twenty-two," I said louder this time through clenched teeth, trying to keep from remembering.

Nothing truly helped though. That day had been burned into my brain. I couldn't get it out. Not the way Daddy looked or how Momma had run past me to the awful scene in the place where our car should have been parked. The horrific sound that had torn from her chest when she saw him in there. Hanging from the ceiling. The green rope—the one he used to tie the Christmas tree to the roof of the car every year—around his neck.

The smell of his favorite meatloaf in the oven would always haunt me. Momma had been making Daddy's birthday meal. We were gonna celebrate it after church. She'd even invited the reverend and his family to join us. I had been looking forward to the buttercream cake she'd made fresh, sitting on the cake plate.

I never wanted to see buttercream cake again. I didn't want to smell it. I hated the idea of meatloaf.

"One hundred twenty-two." My voice cracked this time, and I closed my eyes tightly.

Momma's crying turned into wailing. She hadn't eaten since the funeral. I looked down at the peanut butter and jelly sandwich I had made her yesterday, still sitting outside her door. The bowl of peaches and cream oatmeal I had brought her earlier today was cold now and looked unappealing. The fridge was full of casseroles and pies, but the idea of eating any of that made my stomach turn. That was sad food. It meant my daddy was gone. That he was buried deep underground. That I would never hear his deep laugh, that he would never call me Twinkle Toes again.

"One hundred twenty-two. One hundred twenty-two. One hundred twenty-two."

Momma needed to eat. I should call someone, but who would I call? No one had called the house. I wasn't sure who could help me get Momma out of her room. I wished Daddy were here. When he had been alive, he'd handled all our problems.

"One hundred twenty-two. One hundred twenty-two. One hundred twenty-two."

One

DOLLY

The band was playing our song—or the song I had decided was ours since it had been playing the first time we kissed. Canyon pulled me tighter to him, and I closed my eyes and relished the moment.

Once upon a time, I hadn't imagined a man like him would ever notice me. In fact, I was sure I was going to die alone with an apartment full of cats as my only companions. Not that I even owned a cat, but I had seen it looming in my future once.

Thankfully, time had been good to me—or like Momma said, I had been a late bloomer. A really late bloomer, if you asked me. Canyon had been my first kiss, which was sweet and all, but I was also twenty-one years old. It touched on embarrassing. What girl was twenty-one when she got her first kiss? It was just pathetic.

I wouldn't think about that right now or perhaps ever again. I was on the arm of a handsome man who smelled of cologne and leather—maybe a slight stench of cigarette smoke, but I could overlook that. He overlooked my complete lack of experience with all things sexual. But I knew tonight was the night. We were going to finally have sex. It was about time too. The only thing worse than dying alone with an apartment full of cats was to die alone as a virgin with an apartment full of cats. That had to be remedied.

I'd been waiting patiently because Canyon had said he wanted me to be sure. My comfort was important to him, and that was the sweetest thing I had ever heard. However, today, when he'd picked me up, he had said something about taking me back to his place, and I had known then that this was it! I would no longer be a twenty-one-year-old virgin.

"Fuck," Canyon muttered as his body tensed up.

For a brief moment, I worried that I had stepped on his toes. I wasn't the best dancer, but then when had I been given much time to learn to dance? When one did not have a boyfriend, they didn't get to dance very often.

He stopped dancing, and my eyes flew open to stare up into his rugged, chiseled face. Even the burn scar on his neck, which looked like someone had tried to brand him, was sexy. There was that swagger that few men had, but Canyon had managed to be blessed with it in abundance.

His jaw was clenched tightly as he stared over my head at someone or something behind me. I started to turn around, but his hands grabbed my shoulders and held me in place. He barely glanced down at me, but the brief moment that he did, I saw the apology or perhaps concern in his hazel eyes.

"What's wrong?" I asked as his grip began to hurt me somewhat, not that I would complain.

I wasn't one to draw attention to myself. I preferred not to annoy anyone. My best friend, Pepper, had said that she was going to shake that out of me one day. She hated that about me, but it was just because she loved me and felt as if I let others walk all over me.

"You need to go to the back, call your momma to come get you, and leave," he said in a low voice.

"What?" I asked, blinking in confusion.

Call my momma? To come pick me up at a bar? No way in heck. I wasn't about to send my momma into an early grave. She'd be madder than a wet hen, and it didn't matter that I was twenty-one years old—I was not telling her I was at a bar. I had worked two jobs for over two years to be able to afford my own apartment just to get her out of my business.

"Your momma, Dolly. Call her. You need to leave. Now."

Typically, I would do as I had been told. Not pitch a fit and be difficult. But he was asking something of me I could not do. Not today or in fifteen years. At no point in my life was it gonna be okay to tell my momma to come pick me up at a place like this. I could, however, call Pepper. She'd come and get me.

"Okay," I replied. "But my phone is in my purse, and I left it at the booth with Bolt."

Bolt was one of his friends, he let Canyon boss him around. Which was why he was watching my purse—Canyon had told him to.

"Fuck," he growled.

His body had gotten so tense that I started to apologize for being a problem when he moved me over and then stepped in front of me, shoving me behind him.

I stared at his back, not sure if he now wanted me to stay here or leave.

"You lost, Abe?"

I didn't recognize the threatening sneer in Canyon's tone. I shivered. That didn't sound like the man I knew at all.

"Tread carefully," the other voice replied.

Whoever he was, I couldn't see him due to Canyon being six foot two, and even with my heels on, I was only five-six. And oddly enough, the other guy's first name was my best friend's surname.

"Don't think you can come inside my territory and make threats," Canyon said, holding out his arms, as if to show him something. "This place is packed with Crowns."

A low, amused chuckle came from the other man, and I tried to peer around Canyon's body to see who that voice belonged to. There was something familiar about it. It felt as if I knew that voice.

"Perhaps prison slowed your already-addled brain," the man said in a deep drawl.

I stopped trying to see him then. My heart began to speed up, and my eyes swung back to the leather vest covering Canyon's back. Had he said prison? As in Canyon had been in prison?

"The building is surrounded by Judgment, and the parking lot is filled with the rest. Did you really think I wouldn't come for you when they let your sorry ass out?"

My hand flew to my mouth as I covered the gasp. This was bad. My eyes scanned the area that I could see. Men stood with their hands on the guns at their hips. As if, at any minute, the place was going to erupt in gunshots.

"You really want to do this? After five years?" Canyon asked.

"Yeah, it seems I do," the man replied.

He seemed much more relaxed about this entire thing. Although I couldn't see him, his voice never rose. The tone didn't change. He could have been having a polite conversation.

A gunshot rang out then, and I screamed before grabbing Canyon's vest and burying my face in it.

"The next time you reach for your gun, I'll put the bullet in your skull," a deep, menacing voice said.

Trembling, I closed my eyes tightly, trying to decide if this was a dream, or if I should run for the door, or if I should start asking the Lord for forgiveness now, in case I didn't make it out of here alive.

"Gage Presley?" Canyon's tone made it hard to tell if he was asking a question or not. He seemed shocked. The tremor of fear I detected in his voice didn't make me feel better about any of this.

Who was Gage Presley?

"You were locked up," the familiar voice said with amusement. "Not living under a fucking rock. Surely, you know about The Judgment's connection to the family."

Canyon's arm reached back, and his hand wrapped around my arm. I wanted to jerk it free and run. Maybe scream at the top of my lungs for help.

"I thought it was a rumor."

"You thought wrong," the scarier-sounding man said.

Canyon pulled me around to the front of him, and my heart slammed frantically against my chest. Tears filled my eyes, and I began to silently repent for my sins. There were more than I'd realized when I got started. I had a list of things to ask God to forgive me for. Starting with lying to my momma about who I was dating.

"Dolly?" the other man said.

My eyes snapped up at the sound of my name, and although the waterfall about to unleash from my eye sockets was making it hard to see clearly, I recognized him. It had been years. Six years, four months, and fifteen days, to be exact, but I was ashamed I still knew that. I had tried to stop keeping up with it when I started dating Canyon, but that was easier said than done. It was a habit. I liked numbers, and I often kept count of days when attached to things I liked. A long time ago, that had been Micah Abe.

"Micah," I choked out in disbelief.

That was why I had known his voice. Of course I would recognize it. How could I not? When I was younger, he had been my sole obsession. Not that he cared.

Canyon's arm came around me and pulled me back against his chest. "How do you know Dolly?" he demanded.

The possessive way he'd said my name would have made me giddy if there wasn't a good chance I was going to be shot. Intentionally or not.

Micah ran a hand over his face and groaned in frustration. As if I was in his way and not terrified out of my mind. Why was it again that I had harbored a crush on this man for most of my life? Oh yeah. Because he was ridiculously beautiful, and once, a long time ago, he had stood up for me when some guys were making fun of me at school.

"Let her go, Canyon, or I'm letting Gage put you down before I get what I came for," Micah told him.

I swung my eyes to the other man, not liking the idea of someone pointing a gun in this direction. If I wasn't plumb scared to death, I would have laughed. The man was smirking, and his eyes seemed to dance with merriment. He looked like a model. The kind you saw on a billboard in Times Square.

"It's okay," he said to me. "I don't miss." Then, he winked.

Canyon's fingers dug into my flesh as he held on to me. I whimpered in pain and turned my gaze up to him pleadingly. It felt as if his nails were breaking my skin.

"Did you set me up?" he snarled, glaring down at me.

I opened my mouth, but nothing came out. What did you say when the man you thought you were in love with accused you of something like this? I started to shake my head.

"Dolly isn't involved in this, but she's going to be splattered with your fucking blood in seconds if you don't let her go," Micah warned him.

"Maybe sooner. I have a twitch in my finger," the man named Gage said, then chuckled as if he'd told a joke.

"Did you lie to me? Was this sweet, innocent shit an act?" Canyon asked me incredulously.

There were many things I should be thinking right now. Like how to survive this. But my cheeks heated from the words he'd just shared with a room full of men…and Micah.

"I didn't," I managed to say.

"Last warning," Micah said.

Canyon's gaze was searching, as if he was looking for the answer. He wanted to believe me, but there was doubt. Uncertainty. Even hurt in his eyes. When he shoved me away from him, I stumbled backward and caught myself by grabbing on to a table.

"You've got ten days," Micah told him as he walked over to me and held out his hand for me to take.

I stared down at it, then up at him. Was he serious? He wanted me to just walk out of here with him?

But what other choice did I really have?

"Come on, Dolly," he urged, and the gentleness in his eyes was what had me slipping my hand into his.

He pulled me to him and wrapped an arm around me before turning and heading toward the door. I started to look back.

"Don't," he warned me. "If he reacts, Gage will kill him."

I nodded and let him lead me away. I felt numb as the door closed behind us and we stepped into the abnormally cool spring evening for Florida.

What had just happened?

"I'm gonna guess Pepper doesn't know you've been dating him," Micah said, and I lifted my gaze up to meet the magnetic blue eyes I had once compared to the color of a raindrop.

"No," I admitted. "She's been busy."

He sighed and nodded. "Yeah, she has been."

I turned my head to look at anything but him.

A tall man with broad shoulders, light brown hair so long that he had it twisted up into a bun at the nape of his neck, and hazel eyes approached us. He studied me for a moment, then shifted his attention to Micah.

"You're picking up women? Right now?" he asked him, looking annoyed.

"I'm not picking her up. I'm saving her. She was with Canyon," he replied.

The guy narrowed his eyes. "So?"

Micah tensed, and I watched as his expression hardened. "So, this is my little sister's best friend."

The guy's eyes widened, and he looked back down at me. "Well, damn. That's gonna fuck shit up."

Two

DOLLY

"Here," Micah said, basically shoving me toward the guy with a man bun. These dang heels were going to end up breaking my ankles if I kept being pushed around like this. "Take her in your vehicle."

My eyes swung back to look at Micah. He had forced me to leave my boyfriend, and now, he was giving me to some man I didn't know? I needed to call Pepper. She would be able to free me from whatever insanity her brother was involved in… but my purse was inside the bar.

Crappity crap, crap.

"My purse!" I told Micah. "I left it in there."

He had the gall to look annoyed. At me! This was his doing. Not mine. I opened my mouth to tell him just that, too, but he turned his head slightly to the left and lifted his chin at one of the other men.

"Go get her fucking purse. Take those three with you."

I closed my mouth, not even bothering with a thank-you. He didn't deserve one. This day was supposed to be the most romantic day of my life, and he had walked right into it and ruined everything. All the plans I had made. I'd even sucked it up and gotten waxed. Between my legs! Did he have any idea how embarrassing and painful it was to have someone wax up your privates, then rip it off? Now, that was all for nothing. I would be lucky if Canyon ever spoke to me again.

"Where do you want me to take her?" the man-bun guy asked.

Micah let out another groan and ran his hand through his dark golden locks. Micah had always kept his hair just long enough to be able to pull it back. But he never let it get too long. I hated that I knew that about him. I also knew his shoe size, favorite movie, the way he liked his coffee, and his favorite foods. Once, I had made it my life mission to know all the things about him so I could hopefully use that knowledge to win his heart. Which was a completely idiotic, naive little girl daydream. I had grown up. Thank the good Lord.

"Fuck," he muttered. "Where are you living these days, Dolly?" he asked me. "You still at your momma's?"

I threw my shoulders back and looked him straight in the eye, insulted that he'd think I was still at my momma's house. I was twenty-one years old. Granted, I was a virgin, but I wasn't that pathetic. "No, I am not still living with Momma," I stated matter-of-factly. "I have my own apartment."

He didn't seem impressed. "In Stuart, near your momma, I hope," he drawled, then turned to look at the guy he'd basically tossed me off to. "She can't go back to Stuart. Not until Canyon makes his next move. Pepper will have my balls if something happens to her. Just"—he sighed heavily—"take her to the club. I'll figure shit out later."

Club? Ain't no way I was going to his little motorcycle club's clubhouse.

"My apartment isn't in Stuart," I informed him. I started to tell him where it was when he held a hand up at me, as if I were a child, to shut me up. My back stiffened.

"Doesn't matter. Canyon will know where to find you. You're going to the club until I have time to figure it out."

Before I could argue, the man behind me asked, "Why can't you take her? I'm heading back to Ocala. That's not in my direction."

He chuckled as if that suggestion was funny. "Surely, Levi, you've figured out by now that I don't put a bitch on the back of my bike."

Bitch? Excuse me? I crossed my arms over my chest and glared at him.

"I'll take her," a deep, gravelly voice said somewhere off to my right.

Micah nodded once. "That'll work."

No, it would not work!

"I want to go home. In a car," I demanded.

Micah ignored me and walked over to throw his leg over an intimidating-looking motorcycle. I just stood there and watched as he ignored me. The man wasn't even acknowledging that I had spoken.

"When did you start acting so ugly, Micah Abe?" I asked, my eyes narrowed as I stared at him.

He smirked as he finally looked my way again. The dimple in his cheek still made my stomach do weird things. "Sugar, ain't no woman ever called me ugly."

I rolled my eyes and put my hands on my hips. "You know what I mean."

He chuckled just before the roar of his bike drowned out anything else I was gonna say. The other bikes seemed to take that as their cue, and the entire parking lot became a deep rumble that vibrated the ground under my feet.

"Better go get on the back of Tex's bike," the man Micah had called Levi said from behind me. Even though he was basically shouting over all the dang noise that I barely heard him.

I turned my head to look over at the men on shiny death mobiles. I had been too scared to ride on Canyon's. Momma had said getting on a bike was asking for a funeral. I believed her, but it didn't look like I had much of a choice in the matter. A tall, lanky guy with short brown hair approached me then and held out my purse for me to take.

I reached for it and said, "Thank you," even though I couldn't hear my own voice.

He simply nodded and walked over to an unoccupied bike and climbed on it. Just like the others, he was wearing a leather vest that said *Judgment* on the back, above half of a skull that wore a crown and had angel wings with lightning bolts surrounding it. Fighting back tears from the pure frustration and horror this day had turned into, I glanced out at the men, trying to figure out who Tex was and if this was truly my only option.

A man with dreadlocks and brown hair, bare arms covered in tattoos, and a dark pair of sunglasses held up a hand to me, then motioned with a nod of his head to come on. Great. I was not only getting on a death trap, but the driver also looked like *he* belonged in prison. Perhaps this day could get worse.

My only other option was going inside to beg Canyon to believe me. But I had a feeling if I did that, then Micah and these men would retaliate. I didn't want anyone hurt. Especially Canyon. Sighing in defeat, I walked over to the scary biker. He held out a hand to me, and I stared down at it. He had more rings on his fingers than my momma, and that was saying a lot. Momma loved her jewelry. I could hear her voice clear as day, telling me that I couldn't trust a man who was covered in tattoos and wore rings.

Well, Momma, looks like I don't have a choice, I thought bitterly.

Placing my hand in his much larger one, I let him steady me as I tried to climb on the back of his bike with some dignity. Which was impossible with these heels on. I looked more like a toddler trying to get up on her first tricycle.

When I was finally on the back and felt steady, Tex called back to me, "Hold on to me, darlin'."

I frowned, thinking there was no way I was wrapping my arms around some strange man.

When I didn't do as instructed, he turned more this time and pulled his sunglasses down so that I could see the green of his eyes. "You gotta hang on to me if you don't want to fly off the fucking back of my bike."

Oh. Well, in that case, I guessed I was wrapping my arms around a strange man. I nodded, and the corner of his lips twitched in amusement before he turned back around and revved his engine. I shoved my purse down between the middle of my legs before scooting closer to him and putting my arms around his very hard middle. Sure, I had seen his muscular arms, but it was still shocking. I felt his body vibrate from a deep chuckle, and I winced.

How had I ended up here? Why did I have the worst luck in the world? Why wasn't I more like Pepper? She would have told all of them to go to hell and walked away on her own two feet. Not caring what they said or threatened. My best friend was a force of nature. I was not.

When the death machine I was on pulled out into the pack of other bikers, I closed my eyes, afraid to watch.

My life couldn't end like this. It just couldn't. I had things to do. Losing my virginity was at the top of that list. Yes, I had a list. I'd written down my goals the day I turned twenty-one, and I was slowly checking them off said list. I'd moved out of my momma's house in Stuart, Florida, three months ago and into an apartment in Coral Gables. I was registered to start classes at the University of Miami in a few weeks. I had cut off five inches of my hair; although it was still long, it wasn't all the way to my waist—the way my momma had wanted it. I even had layers in it now. Something she had frowned upon, but I felt it made me look older, sexier, stylish. I still had ten more things on that list to accomplish, but I wasn't sure I would see another day. How tragic would that be?

Three

MICAH

Fucking piece of shit. Canyon Acree.

Five years, I had waited to get back what he'd taken from us, but even more than that, I wanted revenge for what he'd done to my sister. The fucker had been expecting me. His acting sucked. Knowing he had gotten close enough to Pepper to figure out an obstacle infuriated me further. I'd need more protection put on Pepper. She was too damn smart for him, but he had found someone who would work at throwing me a curveball. Someone who wasn't so smart.

The sight of those amber eyes staring at me in shock, blinking, with that perfect heart-shaped mouth of hers had been like a damn slap in my face. Dolly Dixon was all grown up, and she'd turned into the beauty her youthful features had once promised. Not that it mattered. She was off-limits. Pepper would cut off my balls if I touched her best friend.

She'd been protecting Dolly since they had been kids. Pepper was a wildcat that feared nothing, smart, quick-witted, and often terrifying. Dolly was sweet and a touch slow; she smiled easily, and there was a kindness in her eyes that you couldn't manufacture. It was real. The girl was too fucking easy to manipulate, and Canyon had taken advantage of that, knowing I wouldn't take him down when he had something so precious to my sister in his possession.

Bastard.

Now, I was faced with explaining this to Pepper without her taking her own gun and hunting down the VP of the Crowns herself. I wasn't planning on killing Canyon. Just getting the hundred grand he owed The Judgment. If he touched one hair on my sister's head again or even threatened her, then he was a dead man. I'd kill him myself. There would be no need to take Gage Presley with me to do the job.

The sight of Presley struck fear in any sane man who knew the family—or at least who they were. In the South, there were few people who didn't know and respect the family and their power. The Southern Mafia was no fucking joke. They killed without flinching. Their relations with the government went all the way to the White House. If one of them was sent for you, it was bad. If it was Presley, then they wanted you dead. Canyon knew that. I'd made my point.

But then he had made his too.

Snarling in disgust, I pulled into the gates surrounding the club, also known as The Sanctuary. I was the vice president of The Judgment MC. The only one I answered to was Liam Walsh, the president. He wasn't here though. He rarely was these days. He spent most of his time north of here, near his daughter and grandson. They were the reason we had the power of the family on our side.

Liam's daughter had married Blaise Hughes, the current boss of the Southern Mafia. For a man who was also known as the Devil, he would move heaven and earth for his wife and son. The connection had made The Judgment the most feared and respected MC in the South.

I cut the engine once I was parked and got off my bike. I had shit to figure out, but first, I needed to hand Dolly off to someone. It wasn't like I had time to deal with her. She appeared to have more sass to her than I remembered, and listening to a woman bitch right now wasn't on my agenda. First, I had Dylan—a stripper at one of the five adult clubs The Judgment owned—waiting in my room to suck my dick and get the edge off. I'd call Liam after that. He would have to approve me sending more protection over to cover Pepper until this was handled with Canyon.

Tex pulled up beside me with Dolly pressed against his back. Her face was pale, eyes wide, and her lips looked fuller than normal, as if she'd been biting that lower lip of hers, making it appear swollen. Her long, dark hair was a tangled mess. I scowled, realizing Tex hadn't put a helmet on her. If Pepper found out about that, I'd get a tongue-lashing.

When he was parked, he smirked and held out a hand. "Take my hand, darling. Your legs are gonna be a touch wobbly. Don't want you falling off my bike."

If looks could kill, the one Dolly shot me would be lethal. She placed her hand in Tex's, but didn't stop glaring at me, as if she was planning on balling up that dainty hand of hers and planting it in my face the moment she was on solid ground. I wondered if I would even feel it. I'd forgotten how petite she was. Those heels of hers gave her some height, but the girl hadn't gotten any taller since the last time I had seen her.

"I'm calling Pepper to come get me," she threatened. "I want to go home, Micah Abe. HOME. Do you hear me?" Her voice got louder with each word.

I flicked a glance at Tex, who was grinning like a damn fool. She made a sight, standing there with her hands on her hips and fire in her eyes. Even though she was wearing fuck-me heels, she still had to tilt her head back to look up at me. What was she, like five-two? I liked my women tall with legs for days, but I would be lying if I said Dolly's curvy little body wasn't sexy as hell. Not that I would go there. Ever.

"Tell her I said hi," I replied, then looked past her to Tex, who had gotten off his bike. "Take her to Nina. I need to take the edge off, then call Pres."

Tex nodded. "All right," he replied.

"I am not going inside that…that…place!" Dolly informed me. "I want to go home."

Sighing, I turned my attention back to Dolly. "You can't go home. Canyon knows where that is. You're not safe there anymore, Tink. He thinks you set him up. Which is fucking comical, but he's never been a smart man. Now, take your little fired-up ass inside and go be a good girl while I figure out what to do with you." Which wasn't the truth, but what was I going to tell her? She didn't need to know that he had used her.

Her eyes narrowed, and the gold flecks in the amber color looked as if they had caught on fire. "What did you just call me?" she demanded.

"Tink," I replied, amused with this new side of shy little Dolly Dixon. It was spunky, and I hadn't expected that from her. "As in Tinker Bell."

Her eyes flared, and she straightened her shoulders, as if that would make her taller. It was cute. "Is that a jab at my height?"

I let my eyes travel down her body slowly before lifting them back to meet her eyes. "Well, you're not blonde, blue-eyed with a little green tutu on."

Her hands fell from her hips and balled at her sides.

"All right, sugar," Tex interrupted. "Let's get you inside. Nina will have something good to eat, and she's real nice. You'll like her. I swear it."

Dolly barely acknowledged his words as she kept her gaze locked on me. "I'm not hungry, and I don't want to go inside. Call Pepper now, or I'm going to."

She took a deep breath, and I tried real damn hard not to let my eyes drop back to her tits, but I failed. She'd not only gotten some sass about her, but Dolly had grown a rack. That tiny little body might lack length in her legs, but, damn, she had all the right curves. She was a compact little bombshell. Just like every porn cartoon version of Tinker Bell I'd ever come across on the internet. Not that I searched that specifically, but I was thinking I might need to do it later.

Reaching for her purse, she was distracted by her attempt at being threatening, and I snatched it from her hands, then tossed it over to Country, who had been standing behind her, watching the entire thing with an amused grin on his face. He caught it and raised his eyebrows at me in question.

Dolly spun around to see what I'd done with it, giving me a clear view of her juicy, round ass. Yeah, I needed my cock in a willing mouth now. I was too damn horny to deal with my little sister's best friend.

"What are you doing?" she demanded.

"Making sure you don't call Pep until I do. Now, if you'll excuse me, I'm going to unload in a hot, willing mouth."

I strode to the door, opening it up and ignoring Dolly's outraged shout. With a grin, I headed for the stairs. The guys could handle her until I was ready to deal with her.

Climbing the steps two at a time, I could smell the scent of Dylan's perfume. She overdid it with the stuff, but her mouth was like a fucking vacuum from heaven that sucked you dry. I could overlook the other stuff. Even her clinginess. When she got too clingy or acted jealous, I always shut her out until she got over it. I didn't want one woman. I wanted a fucking lineup, an array of choices that came with no strings or commitment.

Only once, when I had been young and stupid, had I loved a girl. I'd almost made the mistake again and fallen in love with a woman who had saved us both by being smart enough to end things. I wouldn't give a female that power. Besides, having them all there laid out for the taking, a different flavor every time, it didn't get much better than that. My life was good just the way it was.

When I had the club's money back from Canyon, then it would be right near perfect. Liam would hand over the control of our biggest club, River Styx, to me. I had plans to make it the best in the southeast.

Shoving open the door to my bedroom, I walked inside to find Dylan already naked, on her knees, looking up at me through her long, dark lashes that the club paid for her to keep. Her platinum hair, which I knew wasn't her real hair color, fell down her back in waves as she tilted her head back and looked up at me.

"You hungry for my cock?" I asked, pulling my gun from its holster and placing it on my dresser before unzipping my jeans.

"Always," she purred, licking her red-painted lips.

"Good. I need to fuck that pretty face hard and pump my load down your throat," I told her.

The eagerness to please me shone in her eyes and it was one of the reasons it was hard to just cut her off. In this world, I needed that at times. The feeling that someone wanted me for more than who I was, what I looked like, my power, my title. With Dylan, I could pretend she did. Even if my feelings for her were nothing more than a small affection.

Four

DOLLY

*Y*ou'll get your purse back," Tex assured me as he led me down the darkest hallway I'd ever been in.

Who painted their walls black? It was like the path to the pits of hell. Or at least what I imagined it would be like. Hopefully, I never found out.

When he stopped at a red door, I was sure this was bad. Nothing good could come from behind a door that color. I tensed as he shoved it open and waited for the worst. What the worst was, I couldn't be positive, but it seemed…*foreboding*. The use of that word from my Word of the Day app on my phone gave me a slight moment of pleasure. The scent of fresh bread met my nose, and following Tex into the room no longer seemed frightening. Hell did not have fresh-baked bread. That I was almost positive about.

The sound of female voices, laughter, and the end of the dark walls brought me farther into the new room—or rooms. It was an open layout with sofas, pool tables, a large flat screen, and a bar to the right while the left had a kitchen with a big wraparound bar with eleven stools. More men in vests were scattered about, as were women.

"Well, who do we have here?" a friendly voice asked.

I turned my attention to a woman setting a loaf of bread out on the counter with oven mitts on her hands. Her dark blonde hair was pulled back in a ponytail. She was older than me, but couldn't be more than thirty. I felt relief at the sight of her, seeing as the other two females I'd seen on the sofas were barely dressed. This one had on a cropped Led Zeppelin T-shirt and a pair of cutoff jeans.

"Nina, this is Dolly, Pepper's best friend. Dolly, this is Nina. She's the angel around here we all love and adore," Tex said, causing Nina to roll her eyes.

"They adore my cooking—that's all," she corrected him. "It's nice to meet you, Dolly. It's been a hot minute since Pepper has stopped by for a visit. Is she here too? I need to pop some of my apple pie in the oven if she is. That girl loves it."

I shook my head, but Tex spoke before I could.

"Pep isn't here. Just Dolly. She was somewhere she needn't be, and Micah picked her up and brought her back here for a bit."

I narrowed my eyes at Tex. Who was he to decide where I should and should not be? He wasn't my momma or Jesus. He had no right to place any judgment on me.

Nina took a slice of the fresh bread and slid it across the counter. "Why don't you stick some food in that mouth of yours and let the woman talk for herself?" she suggested to Tex.

He shrugged and walked over to snatch up the bread.

Nina turned her attention back to me. "Come on and have a seat. I'll get you some of my honey butter and a slice of bread. You can tell me all about it. Micah doesn't make it his mission to save females. I'm intrigued."

No kidding. He hadn't saved me. He'd ruined my day.

I pulled out the stool across from her and sat down. "I wouldn't call it saving. They all seem to have their opinion on that, and I have mine," I told her and added a smile so it didn't sound like I was a bitch.

She chuckled. "You don't say," she replied, then winked at me before slicing a piece of bread, then placing it on a plate to slide over to me. "I'll go get that butter," she added, then headed toward the massive refrigerator.

"Hey, Tex. Come out back and look at this machine that Brick brought in this morning," a man called from the door on the other side of the large living area.

Tex turned his gaze back to mine. "You're good here with Nina, yeah?"

"She's fine," Nina replied as if that was a ridiculous question.

Tex smirked, then turned and headed to the open door. "She's here with Micah," Tex announced as he walked through the room. "Remember that and stay clear."

The other men looked my way, then nodded in understanding as they went back to whatever they had been doing.

"Micah brought a woman here?" one of the half-naked women asked.

"Leave it, Tracy," a man warned her.

When the door closed behind Tex, I was relieved he was gone. I didn't want to deal with any of these men. They all seemed to think what Micah had said was right. They were wrong! All of them.

"Fucking hell, Nina! Why do you torture me like this?" a female asked, then groaned loudly.

I shifted on my stool to see who it was and realized someone new had entered the room through the red door.

A stunning brunette with nothing but a pair of sparkly panties that might have been meant to be shorts and a matching blue bra walked in stilettos toward the counter. Her gaze swung to mine, and she paused, scanning over my body before coming back to my face. "Who are you here with?"

The blunt question took me by surprise, and I opened my mouth to respond, but nothing came out. I wasn't sure how to explain my situation to the woman staring at me.

"She's a guest. Dolly is Pepper's best friend," Nina informed her. "Dolly, this is Amethyst. Ignore her rudeness. She is starving herself today to keep her stomach flat, and that makes her ornery."

"Pepper is here?" Amethyst asked, sounding as if she was happy at the thought of seeing my best friend.

"No, she isn't here. Dolly came with Micah."

Amethyst's head snapped back around quickly to look at me. This time, her eyes widened, and she was assessing me closer than before. I felt nervous under her sudden, intense interest.

"Micah?" she asked, her voice an octave higher.

"Not like that. Christ, Pepper would kill him," Nina replied with a shake of her head. "He brought her here, and I was trying to find out why when you walked in and started hammering her with your nosy questions."

Amethyst didn't even glance back at Nina. She kept her eyes leveled on me. "Are you in some kind of trouble?" she asked me.

I started to say no, but stopped. Because that wasn't the truth. I was gonna be in a pile of hot shit with my momma when she found out about this.

"Not exactly," I replied carefully. "But I will be if Micah doesn't let me leave soon."

My momma could be calling my phone right now, and I wouldn't know it.

"Let the girl eat her bread while it's hot," Nina urged.

I glanced down at the buttered bread in front of me. If I ate that, it would go straight to my hips, but if I was going to die soon and possibly end up in hell, then it might be worth it.

"I'm just curious as to what Micah was thinking, bringing her here. He doesn't typically do the hero thing. And if he was saving her, then why'd he drop her off with you and bolt, leaving her with this bunch of horny bastards?" She waved a hand around the room."

Nina lifted a shoulder. "He knows I won't let anyone touch her. Besides, Tex warned them."

Amethyst didn't seem as convinced. She leaned closer to the bread and inhaled deeply. "Dammit, I think smelling it made me gain a pound. Fuck, that must taste like heaven. Take a bite and let me watch you eat it."

Was she serious right now? I stared at her as she watched me with envy and hope in her eyes.

"Get your bottle of water and a stick of celery out of the fridge and go. You're freaking the girl out," Nina scolded her.

Amethyst sighed and gave my bread one last longing look before walking past me and into the kitchen. "Fine. But I want the details on why Micah brought her here. Nothing interesting has gone on here in months. It's getting boring."

Nina rolled her eyes heavenward, then leaned a narrow hip against the counter and picked up a mug to take a sip. "How long have you and Pepper been friends?" she asked me.

The memory of the day I had met Pepper brought a smile to my lips. She'd been a force to be reckoned with in the second grade, and I'd been the new girl in class, afraid of my own shadow.

"Since the first day of second grade," I replied. "Daddy got a job at a factory right outside of Miami because Momma wanted him home more. He'd been gone all the time before, working as a trucker."

"Where did you live originally?" she asked me.

"Biloxi, Mississippi. It's where my momma was born, and she threatens to move back all the time. But I ain't going, and she knows that. So, she stays in Stuart to be close to me. Having an only child made her a touch overprotective." I didn't add any more of my details about that. The truth was much darker.

"I'd think you would have dropped that thick accent of yours by now," Amethyst said. "I would have never guessed you'd lived around here since you were in second grade. You sound like you're fresh out of Mississippi."

Nina scowled. "Didn't I send you on your way?"

She pressed her plump lips into a pout, then strutted toward the door. I was completely envious of her legs. They were so long. Why had God decided that I was to be a stump? He did unfair things like that all the time. Made me question wasting all my words, praying to him. It sounded like a pointless ritual. He was gonna do what he wanted anyway. I doubted me begging him otherwise would change a dang thing.

"Oh! Speak of the devil," Amethyst said in a singsong voice.

I glanced back at her to see Micah walking through the red door.

His eyes landed on mine, and he smirked. "Take that bread with you, Tink, and come with me. I got some questions I need answered before I call my sister."

"Tink? Well, ain't that sweeter 'n pie?" Amethyst told him with a fake Southern twang.

"Fuck off," he replied, not glancing her way. "You've got a job. Go do it."

"I was waiting on Dylan. Are you done with her?" Amethyst shot back at him.

He nodded. "Yeah."

When he reached me, he leaned against the bar and gave Nina a sexy grin that had once stolen my breath. Perhaps it still did things to me now, but I would like to pretend it didn't affect me at all. Not in the least.

"Can I have a slice of bread, beautiful?" he asked her.

Nina sighed and put her mug down on the counter, then picked up a knife. "Yes. But only if you promise to be on your best behavior with this one. I like her."

He nodded. "You can trust that," he assured her. "Pep would kill me otherwise."

She handed him a slice of buttered deliciousness on a napkin. "You aren't known for respecting things like that," she told him.

"When it comes to my sister, I am," he replied, taking the bread. "Thank you."

She gave him a nod, then turned her attention back to me. "Take yours with you. And don't be a stranger."

I returned her smile and stood up, taking my uneaten slice. "Thank you."

Micah nodded his head toward the red door. "Let's take it to the library."

Library? Who around here read, and what kind of books did they read?

Five

MICAH

I should have called Pepper the moment I brought Dolly back here. I knew that, yet I still hadn't called her. Mostly because I wasn't ready for the drama that was gonna ensue when I did. My sister was a hothead, and when she found out that her timid little best friend had been dating the man who had stolen a hundred grand of arsenal from us while using Pepper as a distraction five years ago, she was gonna lose her shit. Keeping Pepper from going after Canyon Acree herself would be a full-time job. She had her own reasons for hating him.

I finished pouring myself a glass of whiskey, then turned to look at Dolly Dixon standing in the center of the room, watching me. She wasn't pitching a fit like she had earlier. She'd gone quiet on me. Those eyes of hers were wide. And, fuck, how did someone built like that look so damn innocent at the same time? Because she was slow. I had to remember that she was not the sharpest knife in the drawer. I had to be gentle with her. She'd been a sassy little fireball earlier, but I doubted she'd take the information I had well.

"How long have you been seeing Canyon?" I asked her, walking over to take a seat on one of the leather recliners.

Dolly didn't speak or move, so I motioned for her to have a seat on the sofa that was behind her. She glanced back at it, then took her time doing as I'd suggested. Those legs of hers might be short, but, damn, they were nice. I allowed myself the enjoyment of watching her cross her legs as she sat back.

When my gaze finally made it to her face again, I raised my eyebrows in question. "Well?" I urged.

She held her shoulders back and clasped her hands tightly in her lap. The hot pink of her nail polish made the corner of my lips curl. She had always been a prissy thing. Nothing like my wild-ass sister. They were thick as thieves and complete opposites.

" 'Bout two months now," she replied in her thick Southern drawl.

"And you kept that from Pepper for that long?" I asked, surprised.

Her dainty shoulders lifted and fell, drawing my attention to her tits for a moment. "Pepper's been busy with getting the bar ready. I doubt she wants to hear about my dating life. She has more important issues."

I took a drink from my glass. Dolly dropped her gaze to her hands and shifted in her seat, as if she wanted nothing more than to bolt from this room. Most women did everything they could to be near me, yet this one seemed to want to get away from me. My ego was slightly bruised. The Dolly I remembered used to look at me with a worshipful gaze, as if I were the only thing in the world. It had been amusing. I missed that. Then again, if she were looking at me that way now, I might end up fucking her against the desk. Tugging that skirt up and ripping her panties off. Getting a look at that round ass before I...

As that image started to take form in my head, I shook it off. I would not go there. She'd already been taken advantage of by Canyon. He'd pay for that too. Once I had my money. My hand fisted as I thought about the things he'd most likely done to her. Motherfucking bastard.

"When can I go home?" she asked.

"I'm not sure. I need more details. Canyon isn't a good man, Tink. He's a criminal. He's fucking dangerous. He was using you. That much I do know. But I need to know why and what he was after."

Her entire body tensed, and a flash of anger brightened those amber pools as she glared at me. "He wasn't using me. We were fine until you came along," she snapped at me with a fiery look in her eyes.

I almost didn't recognize her. I wanted to chuckle, but I feared it would upset her more, so I held it back.

Leaning forward, I stared at her with my elbows resting on my knees. "Canyon is the vice president of the Crowns. A motorcycle club that is known for their dealings in drugs and illegal arms. They are lowlifes, and this stint in prison he did wasn't his first. Did you know all of that?"

I knew she hadn't by the way her face paled. That heart-shaped pink mouth of hers fell slightly open, and suddenly, all I wanted to do was see those lips wrapped around my cock.

"That can't be," she whispered. "He's always been so sweet and polite. We went on dates, and he bought me flowers."

Even as she defended him, I could see in her expression that she believed me. She was arguing these facts with herself more than anything. Trying to make sense of the man she had thought she knew and the one he had turned out to be.

"And how did he react when he found out you knew me? He hurt you. He wasn't protecting you with a room full of men and their guns drawn. Was he? His first concern wasn't you."

She shook her head, but said nothing. What could she say? Poor girl. I wasn't sure if he'd been using her to get to me or not, but my gut told me he had. It was too close to be a coincidence. I knew Dolly well enough to know she was loyal to my sister. She hadn't known about Pepper's brief relationship with Canyon five years ago. Pepper had been sixteen, and Canyon had been twenty-one. He'd just taken over as vice president of the Crowns. But she hadn't known any of that. In two weeks' time, he had taken her virginity and found a way to break into our arsenal holdings.

"How did you meet Canyon?" I asked her, hoping that would shed some light on this. Give me the proof I needed.

She blinked several times, as if struggling to pull her thoughts together. Hell, she even made the doe-eyed thing look sexy as hell. I'd missed her growing-up transformation. Although I had known it was coming for her one day. It had been obvious when she was a young teen. What had once made her appear awkward and steered boys away now drew men's attention. Teenage boys wanted fast and easy. They didn't know what to do with someone like Dolly, who needed to be taught. Most women built like her with a face like an angel weren't so timid and in need of saving. Dolly Dixon might as well have a sign on her head that said she needed someone to take care of her.

"At a coffee shop near campus. On my way to apply for a job at the library one morning, I stopped in to get an espresso, and he was in front of me in line. He turned and struck up a conversation, then bought my drink and a muffin for me."

Canyon Acree didn't get coffee at college coffee shops. He had been there for a reason, and the idea that he'd been stalking Dolly to learn her schedule infuriated me. Telling her that right now wouldn't go well. I could sense it. She needed Pepper here to explain this all to her. I would rattle her—or worse, make her cry.

"And he got your number?" I asked her.

She shook her head. "No. I don't give out my number to strangers. Not even ones who look as handsome as Canyon," she replied.

"That's good to know. But how did you start dating him then?"

She sighed. "Two weeks later, I was on my way home from my job at Barnes & Noble, and my car got a flat. It was late, and I was trying to find my AAA card to call them when a motorcycle pulled up behind me. It was Canyon. He changed my tire for me, and we talked. Then, he followed me home to make sure I got there safely. It was real sweet," she said with a small smile on her lips.

The fucker had probably been the one to puncture her damn tire. There wasn't anything sweet about it. But I bit my tongue and let her continue.

"I invited him in for a cup of tea, but he said he'd just wait until I got inside. Then, he told me not to invite strangers into my apartment. Ever again. It was then he asked for my number, and I handed it over. He'd been nothing but chivalrous. He called me the next day and asked if I'd like to go to dinner. Then"—she shrugged—"we hit it off."

He hadn't even been slick about it. If Pepper hadn't been so damn consumed with opening her bar, she'd have seen the signs that Dolly had been dating and stopped this. Fuck, this woman needed a keeper. She was a walking target.

Did the fact that he had shown up to save the day when she had a flat tire not register with her at all? And how many bikers with leather vests and tattoos did she see in her campus coffee shop? None. Fucking none. That was how many.

"You're gonna need to stay here until I know Canyon isn't going to come after you. He doesn't trust you, and the man is dangerous. Even if he treated you a different way, the truth is, he is not a good man. The only way I can keep you safe is to put you up in the guest room upstairs. I just need a couple of days. That's all."

Those eyes were wide again with concern. "I can't go home?"

I shook my head. "No. Unless you want me sleeping on your sofa."

She was thinking that one over. There was no way in hell that was happening. I could not sleep in the same apartment as this woman and not end up fucking her. The club gave me enough distraction.

"I would prefer that, I think. I need to check on Mrs. Mildred. She will be needing to pay her bills, and I have to write her checks for her. She can't remember how to do that correctly and gets it all messed up. Last time she tried, she paid her garbage bill twice and forgot her electricity. They cut it off on her, and she thought it was a power outage. She went two days without it, without AC, in the Florida heat. That apartment was like an oven." She paused to take a breath, then started on again. "And who will make sure Harold eats if I don't stop by and bring him a good meal? No one ever checks on him, and his arthritis is getting bad." She shot up to her feet then, wringing her hands. "And Jeremy needs help with his art project. He has to make a replica of the Eiffel Tower, and I promised I'd be home tonight or tomorrow afternoon to help him."

What the fucking hell?

"I can't stay here. I need to go home. Now. I want to go home!" Her eyes began to water as I watched her build herself up into a panic.

"I've already told you, it isn't safe. If you go home, Canyon will come looking for you there."

She threw her hands up in clear frustration. "And if you are right and he is a bad guy, then that puts Mrs. Mildred in danger and Jeremy! His dad doesn't come home most nights until way after midnight, and even then, he's three sheets to the wind! He's just a kid. I have to be there. I have to make sure no one is hurt."

I set my drink down and stood up. "Listen, I can send men to watch your apartment. Make sure everything is—"

"NO! I need to make sure they are okay. I'm not staying here." Her voice cracked then. "Please, Micah. Please let me go home."

Dammit all to hell.

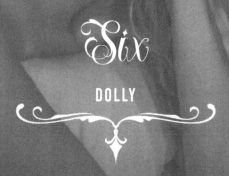

Six

DOLLY

I wasn't sure how long I had been alone in the library after Micah slammed out of there, angry. One minute, I had been ready to bolt, and the next, he had stormed from the room, as if he couldn't get away from me fast enough.

Why was he angry? I was the one being held against my will. I was the one who needed to get back home. He…he was just not getting his way. That was all.

Maybe Canyon was a bad guy, and just maybe, Micah was right, but I knew—I just knew—Canyon wouldn't hurt me. Even if he had been in prison and done the things that Micah seemed to think he had, I wasn't in danger from him. Getting Micah to listen to me was another thing. Especially since I was now sitting in this library, alone.

I let my eyes wander over to the bookshelves. They were full of books, and that impressed me. The men here didn't appear to be readers, yet here, they had a library that I was jealous of. I started toward one of the shelves to see what books they had when the door swung back open. I expected to see Micah, but instead, it was Tex.

He held up my purse. "Got something for you," he replied.

Relieved at the sight of it, I hurried toward him to take it in case he changed his mind. "Thank you," I replied out of habit. Not that I had a reason to thank him. He was a part of all this.

"Don't thank me yet," he replied. "I'm also supposed to show you to your room."

I was in the process of pulling my phone from my purse but paused and looked up at him. "Room?" I asked, not liking the sound of that one bit.

"There was an issue at Toxic Throttle, one of our clubs. Micah had to go handle things. He said to give you your shit and take you to your room."

"He's just gonna keep me here? How long will he be gone?" I asked, feeling the panic rise in my chest.

"Not sure, darling. But you're safe here. No one is gonna hurt you."

I knew arguing was pointless. I had my phone now. I would call Pepper. She'd help me. I nodded and followed him out of the library and down the long hallway, passing the stairs and finally stopping at the second door on the right.

Tex opened the door and stepped back. "Go take a bubble bath or some shit women do. Nina will bring you some food soon."

Pepper would hopefully be here sooner. I nodded and thanked him, then closed the door and locked it. I realized they probably had a key to it, but it made me feel marginally better. Taking my phone, I dropped my purse on the bed and went through my missed calls and texts. Momma had called twice, then left a text about me helping at the potluck dinner at church tomorrow night. She wanted me to make a Crock-Pot of chicken and dumplings. Zander, one of my coworkers at the campus library, had texted, asking if I could take his shift tomorrow morning. That wasn't looking promising at the moment. Then, there was a missed call from Canyon. He'd left a voice message. I stared at the message for a moment before pressing play and listening to it.

"Babe, I'm sorry. I handled today wrong. The shit with The Judgment and Micah Abe is old, and I had hoped they'd let it go. I should have protected you. I should have never let them take you. I'm so fucking sorry. Know that I wouldn't have allowed it if I'd thought you were in trouble. I knew Abe wouldn't hurt you if you were important to his sister. Just…" He paused, and I blinked back the tears burning my eyes. He was admitting it. He knew about my connection to Pepper. He had known who I was to her. "Don't shut me out. Let me explain. I need to explain, baby. Please. Call me."

I sank down on the bed and stared down at the phone. Canyon's name with a heart emoji beside it. What was I supposed to believe? I needed to talk to Pepper. She would help me sort this all out. Make sense of it all. I typed in her name, then pressed Call on my cell.

Three rings, then voice mail. Ending the call, I decided to text her instead.

> I need you. It's a 911 kinda thing. I am currently being held at your brother's club or whatever this place is. He thinks I'm unsafe at home. Call me.

After pressing Send, I waited for the phone to ring or even to see that she had read my text. Neither happened. I tried calling again. Three rings, then voice mail. She would call me as soon as she saw this. I placed the phone on the bedside table and lay back on the bed to stare at the ceiling. Maybe

Pepper would read it and come straight here. Not even call. She'd be so mad at Micah that she would burst in here and take me home.

The knock on my door had me scrambling off the bed and hurrying to the door. Perhaps that was Micah and I was getting to leave. I unlocked it and swung it open to find Nina standing there with a tray of food, just like Tex had promised. Disappointed, I forced a smile.

"Thank you, Nina," I told her, although I wasn't in the least bit hungry. I reached out to take the tray.

"I know you're ready to go, and that food won't make that any better, but I did add a large slice of my coconut cake. It can give you a brief moment of joy maybe." The pity on her face didn't reassure me that I would be sleeping in my bed tonight.

"I'm sure it's delicious," I replied.

It wasn't Nina's fault I was stuck here. She had been nothing but kind to me. I'd manage to eat some of it just not to hurt her feelings or seem ungrateful.

"Try and get some rest. All will look better in the morning."

I started to tell her Pepper would be here to get me before morning but thought better of it. I didn't know how the roles or chain of command worked around here, and if Nina answered to Micah, then as nice as she was, I couldn't trust her.

"I will," I assured her, although it was a complete lie. I wasn't getting any sleep in this room.

"All right then, I'm heading home for the day. My ol' man is working at Throttle tonight. I'll be here in the morning, bright and early. Come on down to the kitchen when you get up."

She didn't live here? Who did all these rooms belong to? No. It didn't matter. I was leaving soon. No need to worry about it.

I nodded. "I will." Another lie. "Good night then."

Once the door was closed and locked, I walked over and set the tray on the dresser. My mouth was dry, so I took the water, but I didn't want anything else. Not even the coconut cake. I checked my phone again, and nothing from Pepper.

Frustrated, I used the bathroom, then lay back on the bed after taking a few long drinks of water. It surprised me when my eyes grew heavy. I hadn't expected that, but then it had been a long day, and maybe resting my eyes for a bit wouldn't be such a bad idea.

Loud knocking on the door caused my eyes to snap open, and I blinked, confused. Then, reality set in, and I remembered exactly where I was and why. Hurrying to get up, I rushed to the door, almost tripping over my heels I had taken off before lying down. I caught myself before I faceplanted and then made it to the door just as another knock rattled it.

Quickly unlocking it, I swung it open to see Tex standing there.

A small smile tugged on his lips. "Getting a nap, darling?" he asked, amused.

I nodded.

"Get your shoes on and grab your things," he said, then stepped back and waved his hand for me to come out of the room.

"Where are we going?" I asked as I went to slip on my heels.

"Your apartment," he told me with a slight curl to his lips. "Seems you've been granted your request."

Relief washed over me, and I let out an excited squeal as I grabbed my phone and purse. Pausing at the door, I stopped to throw my arms around his neck and hug him. It was a reflex sort of thing. I was happy. He tensed at first, and then a low chuckle escaped him, and he returned my hug.

"What the fuck?"

Micah's voice startled me, and I dropped my arms from around Tex and spun around to look at him. He was stalking down the hallway toward us. I took a step back, not sure if I should run now or start screaming. Had Tex been wrong and I wasn't supposed to leave? My stomach sank, and I felt tears start to burn my eyes again.

"She hugged me," Tex said from behind me.

The angry scowl on Micah's face didn't ease my concerns.

"And you were fucking quick to wrap your arms around her," he snarled.

"Heavens to Betsy! It was a hug. And don't you tell me I can't leave here, Micah Abe. I have my phone! I called Pepper!" I warned him.

His eyes swung to me and instantly softened but only slightly. "We need to go."

"We?" Tex asked.

Micah shifted his gaze back to Tex. "Yeah. I'll be taking her after all. Seems you might not be able to handle it the way we discussed."

Tex shrugged. "It was a fucking hug."

Micah ignored him and looked back to me. "Let's go, Tink."

I opened my mouth to tell him to stop calling me Tink but decided against it. He could call me whatever he wanted if he just got me out of this place.

"All right then," I replied with a nod.

It looked as if he was going to smile, but he didn't. Instead, he turned and headed for the stairs. I had to almost run to keep up with him and his long legs, but I didn't mind. The quicker we got out of here, the better. I wasn't going to complain again. I was going home.

When we reached the bottom step, I paused and looked back at the red door. I hadn't eaten one bite of the food Nina had left for me. I should have at least taken the cake with me. Micah wasn't stopping as he headed to the door. I'd have to send her an apology for not having eaten any of it. Not wanting to chance him changing his mind, I sighed and hurried after him.

It was dark when we stepped outside, and the evening air was its usual warm, balmy temp. Micah led me past the bikes to a large, shiny black truck with four doors. He stopped and jerked open the passenger door, then held out his hand to me. As much as I didn't want to take it, I knew I was going to need help getting up in this thing. It was too far off the ground for me. I slid my hand in his, and when he wrapped his larger hand around mine, I tried not to feel anything, but the tingling sensation came anyway. Perhaps some things never changed. I managed to quickly get inside so I could let go of him as fast as I could. There was no good to come of me tingling anywhere because of Micah Abe.

"Nice ass, Tink," he replied before closing the door and walking around the front of the truck to the driver's side.

My face was instantly warm, and I would be lying if I said the fact that Micah had just complimented my butt didn't make me feel slightly giddy. The little girl with a crush was inside, doing a happy dance right now, completely oblivious to the grown-up Dolly, who knew she needed to stop it.

Besides, hadn't I been sure just hours ago that I was in love with Canyon? What kind of person was I turning out to be?

Micah climbed into the truck, and I reached for the seat belt to buckle up, trying not to think about how nice he smelled. Perhaps I just needed a man candle. I clearly had a thing for their scent. Rolling my eyes at my thoughts, I turned my head to stare out the window. Looking at Micah Abe was a massive mistake I would not make.

Once we were pulling out of the gated compound, or whatever he called it, I relaxed slightly. I would be home soon. In my own little space. With my things. I could take a bubble bath and wash this day away with a glass of my favorite prosecco.

"Pep is meeting us at your apartment," Micah said, breaking into my thoughts.

I turned my head to look at him now. "Why?" I asked, still confused about why she hadn't responded to my text or calls.

"Because I stopped by the bar and told her I had you, why I had you, and that I was going to send protection home with you. She isn't expecting me to be that protection because that wasn't the plan when I spoke with her."

I frowned at the idea of needing anyone there to keep me safe from Canyon. "You can't mean you're actually staying with me?"

He glanced at me with a look that said he clearly didn't like the idea of it either. "Not much choice."

"Canyon wouldn't hurt me."

The one hand Micah had on the steering wheel tightened, and his jaw clenched. "Yeah, Tink, he would. If you had just stayed at the club, then this would all be a nonissue."

"For crying out loud," I argued. "He has been alone with me many times. If he were going to hurt me, he would have by now."

Micah sighed heavily. "Just talk to Pepper. I'm tired of this same argument."

His annoyance with me only ignited my temper. How dare he get annoyed with me! I was the one who had the right to be annoyed. Me! Not him!

"As much as I love Pepper, she can't tell me something about someone she don't know. I never introduced her to Canyon. I told you, she didn't know I was dating him. You're making this into something it ain't."

Micah's jaw was working, and I noticed the veins in his neck. He was angry.

Fine. Be angry. Join the club.

I was furious and tired of being treated like a child. My momma already did that enough. I didn't need him adding to it.

"Pepper ever tell you how she lost her virginity?" he asked, his voice tight as he spoke through clenched teeth.

"Yes," I replied, not sure how this had anything to do with me and Canyon.

She'd lost her virginity at sixteen to a man who was too old for her and had used her. She had thought he loved her. I remembered her crying as she had told me about it years ago.

I was a grown woman. I knew better. It wasn't the same.

"The guy who did it was Canyon Acree."

Micah's hard response settled on me as I sat there, staring at him. Waiting for him to say *joking* or *just kidding*. But he said nothing. His body remained rigid. His hand gripped the steering wheel so tightly that his knuckles were white. He was serious.

Oh my God. No. This wasn't right. He was confused. Canyon wouldn't do that.

I replayed that day and all she had said. The weeks that followed and how she was withdrawn, even from me. How I had sat with her in silence and held her hand for hours in my room. Neither of us saying anything. Just sitting there.

"A friend of her mom put him in jail," I said aloud as I remembered her telling me about it.

"Liam Walsh. The man who raised me after my dad died. He's the president of The Judgment. He wanted to be sure I got to see my sister after Dad passed. He and Pep's mom kept in contact for our sake. When it happened, Liam made sure Canyon paid for it and used his resources to put him behind bars for five years."

Micah and Pepper had different mothers. She had said his mom died when he was a baby. His dad had made sure they grew up close even though they didn't live together. Micah would come stay at Pepper's for a week at a time throughout the year and then for a month in the summers. After he turned sixteen, his visits became few and far between. The last time being when we were fifteen and he picked Pepper up from school. He'd taken me, too, and we'd stopped at Sonic to get milkshakes and tater tots.

I wrapped my arms around my stomach as a sick knot formed. How had this happened? The same man had met both of us without the other ever knowing. He'd hurt my best friend, and I'd let him touch me. Kiss me. I felt ill, thinking about it.

Was this a coincidence? Was that even logical? Or had he...

Oh God. He had set me up. He'd followed me. Put himself in my path. But why? To get back at Pepper? Why would he do that? Regardless of the whys, I had thought I was in love with the man who had hurt my best friend and taken something precious from her that she could never get back.

I dropped my head down into my hands and covered my face. I was so stupid. Maybe I deserved to grow old with a bunch of cats. I ought to just go adopt my first one this week.

Seven

MICAH

Pepper was going to hand me my balls for this. She had made me promise to let her explain all this to Dolly, and I'd let my temper get the best of me. Blurting out the truth to her had not been the best idea. She was still hunched over, covering her face, not saying anything. Dammit, I was an asshole, but she had been so insistent on telling me how fucking safe the bastard was.

"This your apartment complex?" I asked her, already knowing it was.

Pepper had sent me the address. I wasn't thrilled about its location, but that wasn't my business. It could be worse.

She lifted her head, and thankfully, there were no tears. Just complete devastation. Yep, my sister was going to kill me.

"Yeah," she replied softly. "Park to the left side. I'm over there on the second floor."

I pulled in beside Pepper's black Mustang and turned off the truck before looking over at Dolly again. She reached for the door handle, and for the first time in my life, I didn't know what to say. Normally, I had all the words when it came to women. I knew how to make them smile, laugh, come while screaming my name. But with this, I was clueless.

"Wait, let me help you down," I told her while opening my door to get out.

She didn't ignore me, but I figured that was only because she feared breaking her ankle if she hopped down in those fucking heels. She held out her hand to me, but I grabbed her waist instead. Damn, it was tiny. My mind instantly went to what she'd look like naked with those hips, tits, and little waist of hers. Fuck, I had to stop that.

But the idea of Canyon's hands on her body pissed me off in ways I didn't want to think about.

I preferred to believe he hadn't touched her yet. That they hadn't made it that far. If they had, then she was handling it better than I'd imagined. Still no weeping or even a sign of a tear.

I let her go when she was steady and stepped back. Her gaze lifted to me, and for a brief moment, there was a flash of something. The kind of something I was used to seeing in women. Oh, hell no. Not this one. She did not need to look at me like that.

I jerked my eyes off her and nodded toward the building. "Lead the way," I told her.

She seemed to remember who it was she had been giving that heated look to and shook her head slightly, as if to clear it, then stepped past me without a word and headed toward the complex. It took every ounce of my self-control not to look at her ass as she walked. She even walked prissy. I'd never met a female as fucking feminine as Dolly Dixon, and I doubted I ever would. There was no way that Canyon had kept his hands off her. I might have to cut them off just to get some peace. Knowing he couldn't touch her again. Making him suffer for taking advantage of her. Dolly was an easy target, and the bastard needed to pay for using her.

I followed her into the building and up the stairs to the second floor. She finally stopped at apartment 205 and pulled out a set of keys from her purse. Before she could put them in the lock, the door swung open, and my sister stood there, looking fierce and relieved, all at the same time. She barely glanced at me before throwing her arms around Dolly.

"I'm sorry you've had such a bad day," she told her.

I heard the sniffle then, and Pepper's eyes darted up to glare at me, as if this were my fault. Well, the fact that Dolly was about to cry might be my fault, but the day in general was not. I had not forced her to date that son of a bitch. I had saved her from him.

"It's okay. Come inside and get off those heels. I've already opened a bottle of your prosecco, and I brought the caramel doughnuts you love from Seventh Heaven," Pepper told her, taking her hand and pulling her into the apartment.

"I'm sorry," Dolly choked out, and Pepper paused to study her a moment.

"You have nothing to be sorry about. Not one damn thing. Do not apologize to me or anyone. Do you understand me? I am here for you. You need me, and I am here to take care of you."

Pepper's eyes darted back up to me then, as if accusing me of something. She was right, of course, but she didn't know it yet. Fucking know-it-all.

Dolly wiped at her face and sniffled again. I hoped she had something stronger than a sweet, bubbly wine. I was going to need it.

Another sob escaped Dolly. Even her crying was delicate. She was so damn fragile that it made a man want to wrap her up and keep her safe. Not that I was going to do that. Not now or ever. But I could admit she had that appeal. One I wasn't interested in. It came with strings and drama.

"I didn't know," she whispered.

I winced. She was going to get right to it. Yep, I needed some whiskey. Even tequila would do.

Please let there be something stronger than wine in this place.

Pepper pulled her back into a hug. "Of course you didn't know. What woman does when she starts dating a man? It's part of dating and life."

Dolly shook her head. "That's not what I mean," she said in a soft, pleading voice.

This time, when Pepper's eyes met mine, they narrowed to slits. I saw the warning there in her gaze. I held up my hands and shrugged. I had done my best. What the fuck was I supposed to do, sit there and be silent while she had defended the fucker?

"Come sit down." She guided Dolly to the pale blue velvet sofa with bright pink throw pillows.

Dolly sank down onto it and pressed her lips together.

"I never would've dated him," she said.

The sorrow in her voice was making my chest feel funny. I needed that shit to stop.

"I need to get my things from the truck and make a run to the liquor store," I said, heading for the door.

"Get me a bottle of Tito's," Pepper called out to me.

I only nodded and didn't look back. I wasn't staying in there for this. Not when I was reacting like I was to Dolly being upset. That shit was messed up. I had to get a drink and shake this off. Maybe I should have let Tex come here, like I'd originally planned. Dolly needed a dependable family man. One who understood her mental limits and need for protection. A churchgoing man. She would never just be a hot fuck.

All that needy, helpless, sexy, feminine shit she had going on? Not what I needed in my life. Not what I liked. I wanted them like the girls at the club. They knew the score. They knew how to please me. That was what I wanted.

Jesus and Tinker Bell weren't my thing.

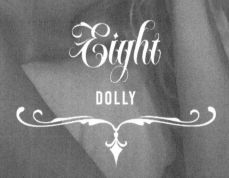

Eight

DOLLY

The moment the door closed behind Micah, I let out a louder sob.

"Stop that. Do you hear me? You did nothing wrong," Pepper said as her arms tightened around me.

I tried to stop the tears, but I felt like a complete fool. I'd been naive and stupid. Why hadn't I questioned it? When had a man like Canyon ever looked my way before? I should have realized something was wrong. But I had wanted to belong to someone like him so badly that I ignored all the signs.

"I'm so stupid," I whispered and bit down on my bottom lip to keep from letting out another pathetic sound.

Here I was, crying for myself, when Canyon hadn't hurt me the way he had hurt Pepper. He'd truly caused damage with her. Taken from her. Yet she had remained strong. Tough. I could too. Right?

"You are not stupid, Dolly Belle Dixon! Do not say that again. I mean it. You are trusting. That doesn't make you stupid. You have the most beautiful traits in the world. You're kind, sincere, thoughtful, giving, and, yes, you are trusting. You see the good in everyone and believe that the rest of the world is just as genuine as you are. But they aren't. And if I could change one thing about you, it would be that you saw the rest of us for who we are. No one is like you. At least, I haven't met them yet."

I leaned back to look at Pepper as I wiped my face with both hands. She had always said those things to me as if I were special. As if she envied me. Which was laughable because I wanted nothing more than to be exactly like her. Wild, brave, tough, brilliant, passionate, and stunning. Pepper Abe was the girl everyone envied. Not me. Yet she always made it seem like that was the case when she spoke of me.

"I should have questioned it," I told her. "His interest in me."

She shook her head. "Stop that. Now. I mean it. I won't hear any more of it. It baffles me that you don't realize how gorgeous you are. Of course a man like that would notice you. You are completely out of his league. Miles out of of his league." She grabbed my chin and held my face so I couldn't look away from her. "For once, listen to me. Believe me. Don't let this bullshit that Canyon Acree did mess with your head. You were making progress."

How had I done this? I always managed to get the focus on me. That was a flaw that I hated about myself. Pepper was the one who had been hurt the worse. This was about her. Not me, yet I had started crying like a baby, and she was focusing solely on me. I was not doing that again.

I swallowed hard, straightened my shoulders, and reached for her wrist, wrapping my fingers around it.

"Let's drink and put this behind us. Forget Canyon," I told her. "Unless you want to talk about it. What he did. I'll listen."

I wanted to be the one to comfort her for a change. It seemed our entire friendship, she had been the one protecting me.

She laughed softly and let go of my chin. "No. That is ancient history. The bastard spent five years in jail. I dare him to come near me. Right now, his life is in danger. There are people who will take him out the moment he steps out of line."

I had met one of those people. I shivered, thinking about the man they had called Gage Presley. He had seemed completely unaffected by the idea of taking a life.

"Let me go pour us a glass, and you can tell me whatever you want to. We don't have to talk about it if you choose not to, but if it will help, then please talk. Get it out," she said as she stood up.

What was there to say? That I had thought I was in love. That he was the first man to treat me as if I was special. I had moved out of my momma's house only a month before I met him. My first chance at getting to experience life without her hovering and controlling me, and I'd messed up that horrifically.

I shook my head. "No. I don't want to talk about him."

She nodded. "Okay then. We will drink, and you can tell me what my brother did and said from the moment he walked into the bar and found you. That I need details on."

"There isn't much to tell," I explained.

She raised her eyebrows. "Really? Why don't I believe you? My brother hasn't seen you since you were a kid. He is a world-class flirt, and you are gorgeous. So, what did my brother say to you?"

My mood sank even lower. Pepper really saw me in a way no one else did. If only I preferred women and Pepper didn't love sex with men so much, I'd have a wonderful relationship.

I shrugged and forced a smile. "He didn't flirt with me."

She frowned before turning and heading to the kitchen. "Either he was being careful, for fear of me, or you didn't realize you were being flirted with. Either way, it doesn't matter. He's not for you. He's a whore. A lovable whore, but still a whore." Her voice trailed off as she left the room.

I sighed and sank back onto the sofa, then stared up at the ceiling. Why was I attracted to men who weren't for me? Maybe Momma was right, and I needed to go on a date with Baker Gilham. He was a nice man. He had a steady job, and he always complimented me. He wasn't wild or dangerous. He also wasn't sexy, but then it didn't seem like I attracted that kind of man.

"I don't normally like bubbly, but this is pretty damn good," Pepper said, interrupting my thoughts as she entered the living room again, carrying two wineglasses full of prosecco.

I straightened up from my slouched position and reached out to take a glass from her. "Thank you," I told her.

She took the seat beside me, then drank from her glass.

"Do you think Micah is actually planning on staying here?" I asked her, hoping he had been exaggerating.

She nodded. "Yes. And you're going to let him. Canyon is dangerous, Dolly. You need protection. If he decides that you are some sort of leverage, then he could take you. This time, it wouldn't be the guy you thought you knew. It would be the real man. He'd use you to get what he wanted out of Micah and the rest of The Judgment. Which I assume is revenge for the five years he spent behind bars."

I looked down at the sofa we were sitting on and couldn't imagine Micah fitting on this very comfortably. I hadn't bought it with the idea of guests sleeping on it. I had found it at a consignment store on sale and fallen in love with it. The small size was perfect for my space and me. Not for a man Micah's size to sleep on.

Before I could voice my opinion, there was a knock on my door. I set my glass down and stood up just as Pepper did the same. She reached out and grabbed my arm.

"It's a little too soon for Micah to be back," she whispered.

I looked back at the door. "I can just look through the peephole," I told her.

She was scowling at the door as if it had personally offended her. There was another knock then.

"Dolly?" the young male voice called out.

I pulled my arm free of Pepper's grip, and she released me.

"It's Jeremy," I told her.

She nodded, recognizing the voice. Glad she wasn't going to argue with me over this, I went to the door and opened it up. Although Jeremy was only eleven years old, he was still eye level with me. He'd had a growth spurt this summer and grown three inches.

"Dolly." He beamed at me. "I came by earlier with my art stuff, and you weren't here. I got worried."

I stepped back to let him inside. "I'm sorry. I ran a little late. Pepper is here, visiting," I told him. "Come on in, and I'll get you a chocolate milk. When's that assignment due again?"

He walked inside and nodded at Pepper before turning his attention back to me. "Not until next Wednesday. It's okay. We can work on it tomorrow."

The hopefulness in his voice tugged at my heart. He was needy for attention, and I seemed to be the only person who gave him any.

"Of course," I told him. "I don't have classes tomorrow, but I do work from nine until five. I got to fill in for someone. But I can make my homemade pizza for dinner." I knew that was his favorite, and unless he ate with me or Mrs. Mildred, he didn't get a hot meal.

He nodded, grinning brightly at me. "Yeah, that sounds awesome."

"School started back last week, right?" Pepper asked.

Jeremy nodded.

"And they're already giving you art projects? Geesh, that's a little harsh," she replied.

I agreed with her, but I hadn't said that to Jeremy. He already hated school. I was trying to help him find a love for learning. I wanted him to do well and one day make a life for himself out of this one. His father was an alcoholic, and his mom had run off three years ago. Since moving in next door to them, more than once, I had taken his dirty clothes and washed them. His father didn't seem to think about his kid needing clean clothing and food.

"Why is the door standing open?" Micah barked as his form filled the doorway.

My gaze snapped up to his, and I inhaled sharply. I wanted to be annoyed with his question, but when he stood there, in all his Adonis-like beauty, it was very difficult to breathe properly.

"Because Dolly has a visitor," Pepper replied, clearly not affected by her brother's appearance. Her tone suggested she'd like to hit him. "Jeremy, meet my brother, Micah. Micah, this is Dolly's neighbor Jeremy."

Micah dropped his gaze to the boy and nodded. "The art project," he replied. "Dolly isn't up for projects tonight. She's had a long day." He walked past Jeremy with a brown paper sack in his hand and set it down on the coffee table.

"Jeremy was stopping by to check on Dolly," Pepper told her brother through clenched teeth.

Micah glanced back at me, then to Jeremy and smirked. "Yeah, I bet. Smart kid."

Not completely sure what he meant by that, I decided getting Jeremy out of here before Micah said something inappropriate around young ears was the best thing to do. I turned my attention back to Jeremy, who was scowling openly at Micah.

"Thank you for checkin' on me. I'll see you tomorrow evening around six. Bring the supplies, and we'll get started," I told him.

He jerked his eyes back to meet mine, then nodded. "Yeah. Okay." He started to turn, then paused. "I'll be home if you need me."

I pressed my lips together to keep from smiling at the protective tone in his young voice. I didn't want to hurt his feelings by laughing at him, but it was cute that he thought he could help me if needed.

"Thank you," I told him. "But Pepper is here, and I am gonna be just fine."

He seemed to relax at that, then headed out the door. I waited until he reached his apartment door safely before closing mine and locking it.

"You're an ass," Pepper said to her brother.

Micah smirked and shrugged. "What? It has been a long day, and Tink needs some rest. Not a horny little kid over here, bothering her."

I gasped in horror at his words.

Micah chuckled at my expression, then raised an eyebrow. "Tink, surely, you know that kid is beating his dick to you several times a day. You're his first crush."

I grimaced. "Micah!"

I did not want to think about a child like that! I swung my gaze to Pepper, who was grinning into her glass. Why wasn't she horrified?

When her eyes met mine, she laughed and then took a drink.

"Jeremy has no parent to take care of him. His father is a disgusting man who is rarely there, and when he is, he yells at him. I make sure he gets good meals and help with his homework."

Pepper nodded her head. "Yes. Because you are one of the best people I know, and he is lucky to have you as a neighbor...but he is a boy, real close to the verge of adolescence, and, well, you didn't grow up around boys like I did." She sighed, still smiling. "Dolly, you are a gorgeous young female, helping him in ways no one else ever has. Yes, he has a major crush on you, and if he thought Micah was going to hurt you, he'd probably try and take him on even though Micah towers over him. He would do it for you. It's cute as fuck."

I stared at her. "He is ELEVEN!"

Micah laughed out loud then. "Yeah, Tink, he is. And at eleven, I was beating my dick on a regular basis. If I got a glimpse of cleavage, I got hard as a damn rock."

"Why are you calling her Tink?" Pepper asked him.

He glanced at his sister. "Because she looks like Tinker Bell but with darker hair."

I rolled my eyes. I was done with this day and Micah Abe. "I'm going to get a shower, then go to bed. Pepper, you know where all the blankets and extra pillows are for Micah if he is still intent on staying here." I didn't wait for a response and walked out of the room.

"Good night!" Pepper called after me.

"Good night," I replied without looking back.

"If you get cold during the night, I'm available for cuddling," Micah said loud enough for his voice to carry, and then it was followed by a laugh. "What? She might need me to warm her up."

"I swear to God, I will throw you out of that window," Pepper warned him.

I reached up and touched my heated cheeks. That was flirting, wasn't it? Or was it just teasing?

Did it matter? Micah meant nothing to me. Not anymore.

Nine

DOLLY

I will not look. I will not look. I continued to chant that in my head as I walked past a shirtless Micah sprawled out on my small sofa. One of his long legs was thrown over the back, and the other foot touched the floor. That did not look comfortable, but the display of so much of his muscular, hard, rippled, tanned skin was making it very hard for me not to stand and stare at him. Take it in. Memorize every inch.

NO! I would not do that. It was wrong. He was sleeping. He didn't know he was barely covered by the blanket that had fallen mostly onto the floor.

Once I made it to the kitchen, I took a deep breath and inhaled slowly. Lord help me, that was not a view I was used to seeing in the morning—or ever actually. Especially not in my apartment. I busied myself with preparing my moka pot with the fresh-ground espresso beans I had bought from

Whole Foods yesterday morning. Caffeine would help. I just needed a jolt to clear my head. That was all.

"Please tell me that contraption makes coffee," Micah said from behind me in a voice that was thick and raspy from sleep.

I tensed and tried to pretend my entire body hadn't tingled from the sound. "Italian espresso," I informed him, then cleared my throat before glancing back.

I was glad I'd spoken before looking. He was still shirtless, wearing jeans that he hadn't bothered to button or zip. The black of his boxer briefs was clearly on display. He looked good enough to eat.

His gaze traveled down my body, then back up as he slowly grinned. "You know, Tink, just because that wrap covers you from the neck to the floor doesn't mean much when it's pink satin and lace. Maybe I should call you Barbie instead. So damn prissy."

I wasn't sure if that was a nice way to insult me or make fun of me, but I wasn't going to dissect everything that came out of his mouth. There was no point in it. He'd be gone soon, and I doubted we would see each other again for another six years. Other than Pepper, we had nothing in common.

My moka pot was ready, thankfully, and I focused on making my cup with a splash of cream, the way I liked it.

"Please make me some," he begged as I took a sip from my cup. "I have no idea how to work that thing."

He was probably exhausted from trying to sleep on my sofa. Feeling sorry for him, I set mine down and went about making him some espresso.

"I can't imagine you slept well on that sofa," I said.

He yawned, and my eyes were drawn to his stomach as he stretched. The way his abs flexed made every private part of my body come alive. He was walking sin. Forcing my gaze anywhere but at him, I walked over to the refrigerator to pull out the supplies for avocado toast.

"I'd have slept better in your bed. Are you offering that? Because I won't say no," he drawled.

I closed my eyes for a moment and took another deep breath. "I suppose we can change places. I'm not as large as you, so I would sleep better on the sofa," I replied while turning back to the moka pot to check on his espresso.

He chuckled. "Now, what kind of man would I be, kicking a lady out of her own bed? I was thinking I'd join you. Just to keep you warm. No touching—unless you wanted me to. I wouldn't mind."

His words brought images to my head that rattled me, and I managed to lose the grip on the moka pot. It slipped from my fingers, clanging and spilling onto the gas eye.

I looked down to see the welt on my skin. The pain from the spilled espresso simmered, but thankfully, the stove's safety switch instantly shut it off. Embarrassed, I was sure my face was the shade of a bright red apple.

"Easy, Tink. I didn't mean to get you so worked up. Did you burn yourself?" he asked, coming up behind me and reaching for my hand.

It finally registered.

Great. Just great.

"You need to ice that," he said, running his thumb over the swollen spot.

I winced, and he made a deep sound in his chest before letting my hand go and moving away from me. Taking the warmth of his body and scent with him. He took three long strides over to the fridge and opened the freezer. When he saw the stack of three bright pink ice packs, a grin tugged at his lips. He took one out, then turned back to me.

"Burn yourself often?" he asked.

I shook my head as he took my wrist and placed the ice pack on my burn.

"I just like to keep them handy if needed. To pack in a lunch box or if I pull a muscle from doing Pilates." I stopped talking as his smile grew bigger. Why was that funny?

"Very organized," he replied, "and pink."

Annoyed by his teasing, I took my hand from his and held the ice pack on my burn. This was embarrassing enough. He didn't have to add to it.

"What did I do now?" he asked.

I turned to the stove to clean up my mess. "You seem to find me amusing."

"I'm not making fun of you, Tink. It's cute."

Cute. Just what every girl wanted to be referred to by a man like Micah Abe. I was always cute. I hated that word.

"I'll clean it up. You keep the ice on your hand," he told me, taking the towel from me.

I let him have at it just to keep from having to talk to him.

He leaned over and started wiping up my spill, and I was too weak not to watch his back flex and move. The tattoos were more like a work of art. I wasn't one who liked tattoos much, but on Micah, they only seemed to make his already-perfect body more appealing.

"Why don't you put up whatever that healthy shit was that you pulled out of the fridge and I'll go get us some real breakfast?" he said as he turned back to look at me.

My eyes snapped up to meet his gaze, and I hoped that he didn't realize I'd been admiring his body.

"There are the doughnuts that Pep brought last night too. I left you three of them, but they are probably not as good this morning."

"I can just eat avocado toast. You don't need to get me nothing," I told him.

He gave me a crooked grin. "I'm starving, and I need a real cup of coffee. I won't go out and get something and not bring you back something too. So, tell me now what you like, or I'll guess."

Fine. At least this would get him out of the apartment long enough so that I could breathe. Get a shower and recover from this morning's events.

"There's a breakfast café two blocks over, called Glory Griddle. It's known for its chicken and waffles. I like the egg white, spinach, and feta omelet there."

His eyes brightened. "I love chicken and waffles," he said.

I caught myself before replying, *I know. With maple syrup.* Or at least, that had been his favorite the last summer he stayed at Pepper's.

I managed a tight smile and said nothing more. He would also like their coffee there. I didn't add that information. He'd figure it out himself.

"You sure you don't want something more filling than that?" he asked me. "Maybe some pancakes?"

I shook my head. "I don't eat big breakfasts."

"All right then. Healthy-ass omelet it is. I'll be back in a few. Lock up. Let no one inside."

Again, I just nodded.

When he left me in the kitchen, I sighed in relief and leaned back against the counter. That could have gone worse, but it could have gone better too. At what age would I stop being an awkward weirdo? With Canyon, I had managed not to be so nervous and clumsy. But Micah Abe got the worst version of me, it seemed.

Just my luck that the only sexy man I could be normal around was a criminal who hadn't wanted me in the first place.

When I heard the front door close, I made my way to the bathroom. No use in standing around and thinking about all the ways I could have handled that better. It was done.

Micah got a phone call once he got back with breakfast, and I was finished eating mine and getting ready to leave for work by the time he was done.

When he walked back into the apartment, he looked at me and frowned. "Sorry that took so long. Had issues with one of our nightclubs last night, and I had to handle some things. You ready to go to work?"

"Yes, I need to go, but I put your food in the toaster oven on warm to keep it from getting cold, and there is an extra key to the apartment on the key ring just there." I pointed at the location beside the door.

He didn't glance back at it. "I'll go grab my food, and we can go," he said, walking past me.

We can go? What?

"You're going now too? You can eat here and leave when you're done or whenever you want to."

"I'm driving you to work. One of the guys is meeting us there and will wait in the parking lot today to watch over you until you get off. I'll be back to get you, but if not, he will bring you back here and stay until I can get here."

Pulling my purse up on my shoulder higher, I thought about my words carefully before saying them. I didn't want to argue more. I'd done plenty of that yesterday, and I was plumb exhausted from it. But I also didn't see how this was needed. Not once had Canyon ever come by my work to see me. I wasn't sure he knew where I worked exactly. Sure, we had discussed what I did, but never details.

"It's a college library, Micah. I'm safe as can be. Most of the time, I'm in the back, pulling the resource requests sent in by professors. They have security and all that."

Micah was chewing with his waffle wrapped around his fried chicken breast in one hand and his keys in the other. He walked past me and opened the door. I was going to be late if I didn't leave now, so I went outside, and he followed me.

"Campus security is a fucking joke. Let's go, Tink," he replied simply and placed his hand on my lower back to lead me toward the stairs. "This is the best fried chicken I've ever put in my mouth. Great suggestion."

I stared up at him, and he winked.

My privates started tingling again. Dang it.

Ten

MICAH

Grabbing the bare ass bent over the bar as I slammed into the newest dancer we had hired at River Styx, I ignored my ringing phone. I was close to coming, and if she kept squeezing her cunt walls on my dick while she moaned like that, I was gonna get off even quicker.

"That's it, sugar," I praised her as Dylan walked into the room and stopped to glare at me.

I smirked and pumped harder. This was a good reminder for her. She needed those often. She liked to think I belonged to her when I had been telling her for years that I didn't belong to anyone.

Reaching for her neck, I grabbed it and pulled her back toward my chest as I jerked my hips with my release. "Fuuuck," I groaned through the pleasure.

Once I was done, I let her go and pulled free from her, then disposed of my condom.

"That didn't take long," Dylan said with a snarky bite in her tone.

I tugged up my jeans and fastened them before sparing her another glance, then slapped the new girl's ass. "Never does when a woman knows how to work her pussy just right."

I wasn't positive about the girl's name, but I thought she had said it was Rachel. Or was it Rama? It had an R—that much I knew. Her stage name was Rainbow. She had a theme going there. Anyway, she was young, but she had some teeth to her. I had no doubt she could handle Dylan.

"Thanks, sugar," I told her before heading past Dylan and toward the door while pulling my phone from my pocket.

"That's it. You just came for a fuck?" Dylan asked.

I paused and looked back at her. "What I do and when has never been your business."

I had to stop letting her suck my dick. She was fantastic at it, but the shit that came along with it wasn't worth it. It had gotten fucking old.

Glancing down at my phone, I saw the call I had missed was from Pepper. Dammit. I glanced at the time, and it was still an hour before Dolly got off work. This couldn't be about her. If it was, then Ringer, the prospect I had watching the library today, would have called me.

I hit Pepper's number and held the phone to my ear while making my way out back to where I had parked my bike.

"Canyon waltzed his ass into my bar twenty minutes ago," Pepper said angrily into the phone.

"What did he say? Did he touch you? Why the fuck was the door unlocked?!" I threw my leg over my cruiser.

"He wanted to talk to me about Dolly! And, no, he didn't touch me. I had my Glock pointed at his head the entire time.

Do I look stupid to you? And it was unlocked because I was waiting on a delivery."

Fuck!

"Were you alone?"

"No. Anson was here, working on the flooring for the stage," she said in a huff.

"Did he pull a gun on the fucker?" I asked, knowing that no matter how much I liked the prospect, if he hadn't handled shit for my sister, he was out. There would be no Judgment patch for him.

"YES! He threatened him and everyone he knows. That is not the point. He said…things. He sounded sincere, too, and that is what worries me. I believe him, but it doesn't make it okay. It actually makes this worse."

"What did he fucking say, Pep?"

She sighed heavily into the phone. "That he is working on getting you the money for the guns he took. He…he apologized to me. And, well, he…I think he has feelings for Dolly. I don't think he wanted to, but he was around her, and Dolly has that effect on people. She's hard not to love. I think she got to him, Micah. And he seemed real upset about how things went down with her at the bar yesterday. He had dark circles under his eyes, like he hadn't slept. I just—"

"Bullshit. Don't be naive. He's trying to save his ass. The family being in our corner has him running scared. Lock your damn door. Keep Anson there with you until you leave. I'm heading to pick up Dolly."

There was a pause.

"Okay," she finally replied.

I ended the call and shoved the phone into my back pocket. I wasn't sure what I was more pissed about. The fact that the motherfucker had had the audacity to walk into my sister's bar or that he had claimed he had feelings and shit for Dolly. He was a criminal. A fucking liar. I had no doubt that Dolly could draw his attention. She had that thing about her that grabbed a man's attention and made him want to own her. But that wasn't what Canyon was after.

I headed to the library to let Ringer know I needed him to take Dolly home and to stay outside her door until I could get there. I needed to handle something first.

Eleven

DOLLY

I normally spent Saturdays at home—cleaning, doing laundry, homework—or sometimes I'd visit my momma. Filling in for Zander at work today had thrown me off my schedule. However, seeing as I no longer had a boyfriend, my night was free, except for helping Jeremy with his art project.

I put the homemade pizza in the oven while Jeremy set up all his supplies on the kitchen table.

"How many of those guys like that do you know?" Jeremy asked me.

Ringer was camped outside my door and refused to come inside. It seemed Micah had ordered him not to come in my apartment. I thought that sounded unfair to him, but Ringer seemed fine with the situation. Micah's orders sounded silly to me. I intended to make sure to take Ringer some pizza when it was finished, as well as take some to Harold. He loved my pizza, but then again, he loved any food given to him.

"Not many," I replied. "Micah thinks I need some protection right now. It's a long story and not important."

Jeremy's brows furrowed in a frown. "Seems important."

Smiling brightly, I walked over to the table. "Well, it ain't. Now, let's get started," I said, hoping he would drop the subject.

"Is it about that other guy who was coming by here a lot?" he asked.

I paused and glanced at him. I'd never introduced him to Canyon, but it didn't surprise me that Jeremy had noticed him coming by.

"It's really not important. We need to get started on this project. If we start gluing now, it can dry while we eat," I said with a smile.

He didn't seem happy about my response, but he nodded, and we began putting the pieces he had already cut out together. While I held them in place, he glued them. I asked about his classes and the girl he had mentioned who was new this year. After a little prodding, he began chatting away, seeming to forget about the biker standing guard outside my apartment.

When the pizza was ready, I sliced him a large piece and made him a glass of chocolate milk before preparing some to take to Ringer and Harold. Telling him I would be right back and to get another piece if he needed it, I headed for the door with my two plates of pizza and a bottle of water tucked under each of my arms.

When I stepped outside, Ringer was leaning against the wall, texting on his phone. He lifted his head and looked at the pizza, his eyes lighting up before meeting mine.

"Hungry?" I asked, handing it to him.

He took it. "Yeah, that looks great. Thanks."

I took a water and gave that to him too. "Enjoy. I have more if you are still hungry when I get back."

"Where are you going?" he asked, straightening his stance, suddenly alert.

"Just to walk this down to a friend. He is one block over. No need to go with me."

He smirked. "You go. I go."

I sighed and shook my head. "Eat your pizza while it's hot."

He picked the large slice up and folded it, then placed the water and plate by his feet. "I'll eat while we walk."

"Seriously?" I asked, frustrated.

He nodded. "Yep."

"Fine. Come on then."

We walked in silence the small amount of time it took to find Harold. He was sitting on an upturned plastic crate with his harmonica, playing an upbeat tune, when he spotted me approaching. A smile lit up his face as he lowered the instrument from his mouth.

"Got me somethin' good, do ya?" he asked when I reached him.

I held out the pizza to him, wishing I could do more for him than stopping by with food. "My homemade pizza," I replied.

"That just might be my favorite," he told me as he took the pizza from my outstretched hands, then raised his shaggy white eyebrows as he looked behind me. The way his mouth tightened into a firm line made it clear he wasn't happy about Ringer following me.

"Harold, this is, uh, well, this is my friend's…uh, friend. Ringer," I explained.

"Friend's friend, is it?" he asked, still studying Ringer closely. "Sweet girl like you ought not to have friends like that. Ain't right. You got the world at your feet."

I gave Harold's arm a gentle, reassuring squeeze. "It's Pepper's brother's friend. I assure you, he is just here to protect me." I stopped then as his eyes narrowed.

"What you need protecting from?" Harold asked.

Why had I said that? Explaining my way out of this one was going to take time I didn't really have. Not with Jeremy waiting on me in my apartment.

"It's overkill," I assured him. "I don't think I need any protecting, but a guy I was dating turned out to be not such a good man. Anyway, all is well. I promise. You eat that pizza. And where is the blanket I brought you?"

His concerned frown didn't ease. "It's folded up real nice under my box here. I like to keep it clean until it's time for bed."

"Good. Well, Jeremy is back at the apartment, needing help with an art project. I have to head back, but I'll make sure we have time to chat next time."

He nodded. "And you let me know if'n these boys protecting you step out of line." His eyes were locked on Ringer, making sure his threat was clear. It was sweet really.

Harold was sixty-three, but living on the streets the past fifteen years made him appear closer to eighty. He had arthritis something awful and refused to take any of the medications I had brought him, saying that taking pills was what had gotten him here.

"Enjoy your pizza," I told him and wished he'd take money, but I already knew he wouldn't. I'd tried too many times to offer it to him.

"Always do," he assured me.

Turning, I glanced up at Ringer, who was grinning like an idiot. Nothing about this was funny. I shot him an annoyed glare before starting back to the apartment.

"You feed old homeless men and help kids with homework." He chuckled behind me.

"Why is that amusing to you?" I asked, not giving him the satisfaction of a scowl.

" 'Cause it just is."

Rolling my eyes, I walked as fast as I could back to the apartment. It wasn't like I was trying to feed all the homeless in Miami. I would if I could, but that would be an impossible task. Harold was special.

I'd met him the week I moved in. I had been walking home a little late after getting lost in a book I was reading at the burger place just a mile from my apartment. Some young guys were calling out to me from their car and following me slowly. I was right near ready to take off running and screaming. Promising God that I wouldn't do this again if he just got me out of this mess.

Then, Harold came out of nowhere, waving a gun, and yelled at the boys that he'd shoot all their sorry asses if they didn't go on. He scared me a touch, but then he'd explained the gun was a toy but a real good replica. He had walked me the rest of the way, and I'd found out that he'd been in the Army. Served in the Vietnam War, and due to some PTSD he'd gotten, he'd become an alcoholic and lost his wife, and his only son had been killed in a car accident two days after he turned sixteen.

His story was tragic, and it broke my heart that he was so alone in the world. So, yes, I fed Harold, and I checked on him. He deserved to be cared about too.

We made it back to the apartment, and I was barely inside when I heard Micah's voice, followed by Jeremy's laughter. I froze for a moment, then hurried to the kitchen.

Micah was busy holding a small square sheet of foil while Jeremy was working on covering the structure we had built with another square. Micah's eyes lifted to meet mine, and then he gave me a crooked grin.

"Hey, Tink."

I paused, looking from Jeremy to Micah, trying to make sense of the situation.

Jeremy glanced back at me. "Micah is helping me. You can eat."

"When did you get here?" I asked Micah.

"Almost right after you left," he replied. "Ringer texted that you were feeding the homeless, so I thought I'd help Jeremy out."

Jeremy's pizza was half eaten on his plate.

"You haven't finished your pizza," I pointed out.

He took the next piece of foil from Micah. "It's okay. I'm almost done with this, and I can take it with me."

This was so odd. I stood there, trying to make sense of it. The last time Jeremy had seen Micah, he hadn't liked him. I hadn't been gone but maybe ten or fifteen minutes. How had things taken a complete one-eighty in that amount of time? Something wasn't right, but I couldn't put my finger on it.

"I'm really hoping there is enough of that pizza for me too. Smells amazing," Micah said as he took a piece of foil and started wrapping the tower too.

I had another one made up in the fridge that I hadn't cooked yet. I'd thought about Micah when I did it, but I hadn't wanted to assume he would be here in time to eat dinner. It was a Saturday night, and…well, he was Micah. He had things to do on Saturday nights, unlike me.

I cleared my throat and decided I would figure this out later. "Yes, I have another one ready to put in the oven. I'll, uh, do that now."

I didn't wait for him to respond, but went about busying myself so as to not think about how he looked right now, bent over a model of the Eiffel Tower, helping Jeremy finish it up. The only thing that even remotely made sense right now was that I had fallen and hit my head somewhere. Because this was not something one would ever expect to see Micah Abe doing.

By the time I had the oven heated and the other pizza slid inside, Jeremy had announced they were finished and brought his plate and cup to put in the sink.

"Thanks for your help and dinner," he said brightly.

Yes, something was off. This felt like the twilight zone.

"Uh, yes, of course. It turned out great," I said to him. "Do you want to stay for some more pizza?" I asked him.

"No. I'm good." He nodded his head toward the pizza on a napkin he'd left on the table. "I'll take that with me. See you later, Dolly."

I watched as he walked back over to the table and picked up his pizza.

"I'll carry the Eiffel Tower," Micah offered.

"Thanks!" Jeremy said, seemingly happy about it.

Well, all right then. Whatever. Men of all ages confused me, it seemed. I was clueless, or I was missing something. Either way, I was going to let it go. Jeremy seemed happy enough.

Micah took the tower and followed Jeremy, but glanced back at me and winked before leaving the room. I stared at the door for a few moments before shaking my head and walking over to the fridge to get out a bottle of prosecco.

I considered texting Pepper to tell her what had just happened and get her opinion on it, but decided against bothering her. I had already distracted her enough from the bar this weekend.

Twelve

DOLLY

Carrying the pizza into the living room, I set it on the coffee table. I could feel Micah watching me from the sofa he was currently leaning back on, scrolling through Netflix. Before I could straighten back up, he leaned forward and took a slice.

"Damn, this looks good," he said, then took a bite.

Refusing to watch him chew because even Micah could make eating sexy, I turned and headed back to the kitchen to get the bottle of prosecco and my glass. Pausing, I glanced over at the whiskey that Micah had bought last night and figured it would be rude not to take it in there in case he wanted more. He already had a glass with some in it, but I didn't want him to choke on his pizza.

With a sigh, I picked it up and went back to the living room. His suggestion that we eat in there and watch a movie had sounded kinda nice. Even if he made me a little nervous.

When Micah looked at me, I felt like that awkward girl I had been. The one that was still inside me. My appearance might have changed, but it hadn't changed much else.

Placing the bottles beside the pizza, I sat down with little room between us because this sofa was not that big. I'd bought it, thinking it was perfect for me. Micah made it look even smaller than it was. The only other guy who had sat on this sofa was Canyon, and that had been only a handful of times.

Shoving thoughts of him aside, I spread out a napkin in my lap and then reached for a slice of pizza. When I lifted it carefully to my mouth to take a bite, I felt Micah's gaze on me. I lowered the pizza and turned to look at him. He was smirking. What was so funny? I raised my eyebrows, feeling slightly annoyed that he could make me so self-conscious.

"Are you always so prim?" he asked me.

"Are you always so annoying?" I shot back at him.

His lips curled into a full-blown smile. "You know, Tink, I think you're the only female who finds me annoying. But then I doubt you really mean it."

I narrowed my eyes at him, hating that he was right. "You're wrong there. Pepper thinks you're annoying."

He chuckled. "Little sisters don't count. And I wasn't making fun of you. It's cute. That proper, prissy shit you do."

Cute. If he called me cute one more time, I was going to shove my pizza in his face. It was grating on my nerves.

"Just stop talking," I said, turning my attention back to the television.

"Ouch," he drawled, but I didn't respond.

Instead, I took a bite and started to chew.

I expected him to talk some more and continue to say things that made me angry, but instead, he started searching the movies on Netflix again. I watched as he went past several movies that might be good when he finally stopped at one.

"You good with this one?" he asked.

I nodded, not looking at him, then picked up my glass and drank down the rest of the bubbly inside of it before reaching to pour myself more. If I was going to watch an entire movie with Micah Abe, I needed help relaxing.

He clicked it, set the remote down, then took another slice from the table. I was finished with mine and used the napkin in my lap to clean my hands, then folded it neatly and placed it on the coffee table before settling back with my glass.

It wasn't until I drank all that I had and was considering pouring more that I felt its effects. Turning, I looked over at Micah, who shifted his gaze from the television to me.

"Don't you have better things to do on a Saturday night?" I asked him.

His eyes danced with amusement. "I can't say that I do, Tink."

I didn't want to smile, but my lips did so anyway. Dang them. "You're lying," I replied.

He took a drink from his glass, not taking his gaze off me. "Why would you say that?"

I threw out a hand and waved it around the room. "This isn't very exciting for you."

He shrugged. "It's enjoyable though."

Enjoyable. That was a good thing. He was enjoying himself.

His hand reached over and took mine. My gaze dropped to see his thumb brush over the small red welt that the espresso had left this morning.

"You want me to get an ice pack?" he asked.

I shook my head, not sure I could form words. Micah grinned, then lifted my hand to his mouth and brushed his lips over the tender flesh. The butterflies in my stomach morphed into something much more intense. They were more like a bunch of crazed seagulls.

"You even smell sweet," he murmured against my skin.

I was sure I might just pass out right now. Micah Abe was kissing my hand—or as close to kissing as one could get—and telling me I smelled sweet.

"You sure you don't want me to get you one of those pretty little pink ice packs? I don't like the idea of you being in pain."

Good Lord almighty, had I fallen asleep, or was this really happening?

I started to shake my head when a loud knock rattled my door.

"Dolly, babe. Open up!" Canyon called from the other side.

Oh no. This was a bad thing. A real bad thing.

Micah dropped my hand and shot up from the sofa.

I scrambled to follow him as he started stalking to the door. He was almost there when I managed to wrap my hands around his arm to attempt to stop him.

"Micah, wait!" I begged, not sure what would happen if he opened that door.

"Let go, Tink," he demanded.

"DOLLY!" Canyon shouted from the other side of the door. "You're not answering my calls or texts. Talk to me, baby."

Micah's eyes locked with mine. "He's called and texted you?" he asked me in an accusing tone.

"We were dating," I exclaimed. "I didn't respond. You heard him." I didn't like the way he was looking at me, as if I had done something wrong.

He jerked his arm free, and his hand went to his back, just under the leather vest he was wearing. Fear sliced through me as he pulled out a gun. Panicking as tears filled my eyes, I didn't reach for his arm this time. Guns terrified me.

"Micah, don't, please," I begged.

His jaw clenched, and it only made the perfect angles of his face appear sharper. "I told him to stay the fuck away from you," he said through clenched teeth. "He was using you, Dolly. What part of that do you not understand?"

Even though I'd already known this, it still hurt to hear him say it. I'd loved two men in this world—or at least, I thought I had. Micah had been the first and Canyon the second, but then with Micah, I had been too young. With Canyon, I had been…blinded.

"Just let me talk to him. Do you have to get the gun out for that? It's a touch too much, don't you think?"

"Go to your bedroom and lock the door," he clipped out.

They were only words, but the memory came flooding back with it. I closed my eyes tightly, fighting it off.

"One hundred twenty-two," I whispered. "One hundred twenty-two."

Another loud knock. "Dolly! Come on, baby. Please."

This was not happening. There was no gun. I wouldn't lock myself in my bedroom.

"One hundred twenty-two."

"Tink? You okay?" Micah asked as his hand touched my face.

I didn't open my eyes. The lump was back. Choking me.

"Dolly, baby, I'm gonna break down the door if you don't answer me," Canyon warned.

Micah's hand left me, and by the time I could get my eyes open, he moved to unlock the door and was swinging it open with the gun in his hand, pointed at Canyon. I was frozen and unable to even shout out a warning. Canyon's eyes swung from Micah's gun to me. He didn't even flinch at the fact that Micah was prepared to kill him.

"Go to your room, Tink," Micah said in a softer tone this time.

I didn't move. *One hundred twenty-two, one hundred twenty-two, one hundred twenty-two.*

Canyon held up both his hands. "Not here to fight with you, Abe. I just need to talk to Dolly."

Micah took a step toward him. "You were told to stay the fuck away from Dolly. You're not gonna use her the way you did my sister. It won't be prison next time."

One hundred twenty-two, one hundred twenty-two, one hundred twenty-two.

The threat in his words didn't even make Canyon flinch. Me, however? I was struggling to take a deep breath. It felt as if someone had me by the throat, tightening slowly.

One hundred twenty-two, one hundred twenty-two, one hundred twenty-two.

"Baby, listen, it's not like that. Not anymore. Maybe it was at first, but…then I got to know you. It changed. I swear." He pleaded as he ignored Micah.

Not wanting anything to happen to him and very close to a complete mental shutdown, I knew I needed him to leave so Micah would put that gun away.

"Just go." The sound of my voice sounded foreign to my ears.

One hundred twenty-two, one hundred twenty-two, one hundred twenty-two.

The pain reflected in Canyon's gaze only made the difficulty to breathe worse. I believed him. Why couldn't Micah? Was it so hard to believe that Canyon could have feelings for me? That he could love me? Maybe it was. My father hadn't loved me enough to stay. There had to be something wrong with me. I had always feared there was. I wasn't good enough.

One hundred twenty-two, one hundred twenty-two, one hundred twenty-two.

"You're scaring her," Canyon said, glaring at Micah now. "She's terrified. Look at her. Jesus, Abe, put the damn gun down."

"Leave before I put you down," Micah replied in a cold, hard voice that was nothing like him.

Canyon turned his focus back to me, his expression softening. "I'll prove it to you. I swear I will. This ain't over."

One hundred twenty-two, one hundred twenty-two, one hundred twenty-two.

He'd hurt Pepper. I could never forgive him for that. But there was a part of me that had thought I was in love with him just a few days ago. That part was struggling with all this. That part wanted to be enough for someone to love. I wanted to believe someone would love me enough to stay with me.

One hundred twenty-two, one hundred twenty-two, one hundred twenty-two.

"I'm gonna walk away, baby," Canyon said softly. He lowered his hands. Then, with one last look my way, he did as he'd said.

My entire body felt numb when Micah closed the door harder than necessary.

"He's a lying sack of shit," Micah swore.

Canyon had hurt Pepper. Even if he was kind to me, even if he had come here to fight for me, it didn't change the past. I couldn't forgive him for what he'd done to her. I knew people could change, and maybe he had, but it made no difference to me.

Micah put his gun back in the holster as he watched me.

"Are you okay?" he asked, taking a step toward me.

I took a step back, needing my space. Right now, if someone touched me, I was sure I would fall apart. I was too close to the edge now. The number *one hundred twenty-two* was still replaying over and over again in my head.

I held up both my hands and nodded. "I'm fine."

"You're pale, Tink," he said in a gentle tone. "I'm sorry about the gun."

I nodded again and took another step away from him. From the door. From all that had just happened. Going back to the living room to finish the movie seemed impossible now. My emotions were all over the place, and I needed to be alone.

"I'm going to bed," I said simply and left him there, watching me walk away.

One hundred twenty-two, one hundred twenty-two, one hundred twenty-two.

Thirteen

MICAH

Leaning against the wall outside Dolly's apartment, I was real fucking glad I'd thrown out all my emergency cigarettes. My five months without one would have come to a screeching halt. Lifting the bottle of Jack to my lips, I took a long pull and let the warmth heat up my throat. It did little to ease the anger rolling through me. Canyon Acree had always been a bastard, but tonight, he'd been real damn convincing.

The gun was my fault though. I'd scared the shit out of her. The urge to go after her when she walked away had been hard to fight. I didn't trust what I'd do if I got my hands on her again. The terror in her eyes should have never been put there. Canyon should have stayed the fuck away. Pepper was right. There was a chance that bastard had developed some feelings for Dolly. Not that it mattered.

I was here to protect her and get back what had been taken from me. This shit show hadn't been anticipated though. If

Canyon was going to be persistent with Dolly, things could get worse. I hadn't expected his play tonight. Pulling out my fucking gun in front of her was something I didn't think I could do again. The look on her angelic face was seared into my brain. It had fucking hurt my chest. What was up with that bullshit?

The footsteps on the stairs were heavy, and I straightened, waiting for Brick, who I had called to come take my place. I needed to go prepare for Canyon's next moves and make sure Dolly was safe from coming in contact with him again. Not to mention, I needed to get some distance from her. Right now, I wanted nothing more than to go back in there and wrap her up in my arms, assure her that she was safe, and fuck the hell out of her. Things that would not happen. Which was why I had to leave.

When Brick made it to the top step, his eyes locked on me. "She kick you out?" he asked.

I shook my head. "No. I needed to cool off. She's gone to bed."

Brick glanced around the place. "Not the best part of town."

"I know," I grunted, not wanting to think about that. I couldn't save Dolly from everything, and I didn't want the job. But, dammit, someone needed to. "Not sure if he's stupid enough to come back here, but the way he was begging her to believe his lies, I wouldn't be surprised."

Brick nodded. "I'll handle him if he does."

Running my hand through my hair, I looked back at her door. "She's naive," I told him. "Sweet as sugar, but she's... slow," I explained. I hated saying it.

When she had been younger, it had been obvious she wasn't that sharp. But now, sometimes, when she looked me in the eye, I saw something there that I hadn't years ago. She didn't seem that slow anymore, and maybe I was off about that. Regardless, she was too gullible.

"Slow?" he asked as his brows drew together.

I nodded. "Yeah. She thinks he loves her. She clearly hasn't had much experience in the matters of men."

Brick looked as if he found that hard to believe. "That doesn't make her slow. It makes her female, and we both know females are a helluva lot sharper than we are. They sit on a pot of gold, and they know it."

I smirked and shook my head. "Not all women."

He tilted his head and grinned. "You sure about that?"

I wasn't going to stand here and argue about the intelligence of men and women. "I need to go. Stay outside the apartment so you don't scare her and don't kill anyone. Call me if Acree shows back up."

"I got this. You can go on," he assured me.

I handed him the bottle of whiskey. "Here. Just don't get shit-faced."

He took the bottle. "Not enough in here to do the job."

I glanced over at the kid's apartment door. I'd promised him a Nintendo Switch if he left us alone tonight. It had worked brilliantly, but my night had gone to shit. I'd been looking forward to a movie with Dolly. I wasn't digging into that too deeply. I also wasn't going to think about the fact I'd kissed her hand. If Canyon hadn't shown up, I wasn't sure what else I'd have kissed.

It was the fact that I couldn't fuck her. The off-limits thing was just making her more tempting. That had to be all this was.

I'd keep my distance. Just call and check in on her. Ringer and Brick could take turns coming over and staying outside her door. I didn't need to be inside that apartment with her anyway. No fucking good would come from that.

Fourteen

MICAH

Sitting on my bike, I listened to the phone ring as I held it pressed to my ear.

"Hello?" Dolly replied in a clipped tone, making me smile.

"Good morning to you too, Tink. You sound chipper."

I could almost see her frowning.

"What can I do for you, Micah?"

Suck my cock, but I wasn't about to suggest that. She'd tell Pepper, and then I'd have my sister to deal with.

"Just checking on you. Seeing if you're feeling better this morning."

"What, after you pulled a gun on a man at my door last night? Yes. I am peachy keen. Thanks for asking."

Damn, I liked it when she was a smart-ass.

"About that, I'm sorry. I shouldn't have done it. I scared you, and I feel real bad about it." That shit wasn't a lie. It had kept me up last night, but I wasn't about to admit that.

She sighed. "Okay."

"That's all I'm getting?"

"What would you have me say?"

"Oh, I don't know. *I forgive you* might be nice."

She let out a small laugh. "I forgive you. Better?"

Grinning, I crossed one arm over my chest and settled in. I wasn't in a real rush to get off the phone, I decided. I was enjoying this. "Maybe. What about you offer to let me come sleep in your bed and keep you nice and warm tonight? That might make it all better."

"I'mma say, hard pass, Micah Abe."

"Ouch. Come on, Tink. You won't even give my cuddling offer a chance?"

Another laugh. "No, I won't. I wasn't born yesterday. Now, I need to get to work. If that is all you called for, I gotta go."

I didn't want to let her go, but I had no other excuse to keep her on the phone. "Have a good day, Tink."

"You too, Micah."

Two days later, I walked into church, pissed off about so many things that I wasn't sure where to start. Liam sat at the head of the table, and Jars, Brick, Butch, and Grinder sat on the right side while Country and Tex sat on the left. I was the last one here.

"Glad you could join us," Tex drawled sarcastically, leaning back in his chair with a cigarette clenched between his teeth.

"Fuck off," I snapped before pulling out my chair to Liam's direct left and sat down.

"Someone has his panties in a wad," Grinder replied with a smirk.

"Dylan giving you hell over Dolly?" Country asked me, grinning.

"I don't give a fuck what Dylan says or does," I snarled, annoyed with the entire conversation.

"And I don't give a fuck about Micah's lineup of females," Liam said. "What I do give a fuck about is Canyon Acree and the one hundred grand he owes us."

"It's been four days. I gave him ten," I told him.

"Why exactly did you decide on ten?" Liam scowled.

"Told you, Pres, Acree had Pepper's best friend with him," Brick said. "Micah was a little thrown off by it."

Which Liam would know if he spent less time in Ocala with his grandkid and more time here. I didn't say that though. Wasn't my place.

"That's the girl we have Ringer guarding?"

"And me," Brick added. "But, yeah, Ringer is there right now."

"Why ain't Micah over there, babysitting, seeing as it's Pep's best friend?" Jars asked, leaning his beefy arms on the table.

" 'Cause she's pretty as a peach and Micah wants to fuck her," Tex said, grinning.

"I don't want to fuck her," I corrected him, although that wasn't completely true.

I'd about decided I might be wrong about her being slow. She wasn't like I remembered when she had been younger. She had a quick wit I hadn't expected. She didn't stare at me silently anymore either.

"I say we shorten the ten days. Might as well make it seven for shits and giggles. I want to hurt the son of a bitch," Grinder suggested.

"You seen the fucking news? Another hurricane formed, and we're in the cone. Be a few days yet though before it lands," Brick told him. "Probably don't want to start any wars when we might need to be boarding up and prepping for a full house here soon."

"When are we not in the cone?" Tex asked. "Tis the fucking season. No need to get worked up over it. Let's go find the bastard and end this bullshit. If Dolly wants to mess around with him when we're done, that's on her."

"This hurricane is promising to be a big one," Brick said.

"We will wait and see what the hurricane is gonna do, and then we hunt him down and get our money, or we send in the family. He's been warned," Liam said. "Now, what's the update on Toxic Throttle's refurb? And has the case been settled with that bitch who was claiming sexual assault when she was caught taking from the register?"

I watched Tex take in another long pull from the cigarette and fought the urge to reach over and snatch it from his hand and inhale. I was ready for church to be over. I had my own list of shit to handle. Starting with one of the dancers claiming she had gotten knocked up by a prospect and demanding the club pay for her abortion.

I knew the first thing I was going to do when I walked out of here was call Dolly. I was finding myself needing to hear her voice, and I wanted to believe it was just because she was important to Pepper and nothing more. If I was honest with myself, I liked the sound of her voice, and listening to her talk soothed me. I was keeping my distance, but I found myself calling her more often than I should.

Last night, I'd talked to her on the phone for far longer than necessary. Just listening to her go on about her job, Mrs.

Mildred, and her attempt to get Harold to sleep on her sofa had distracted me from everything else.

She made me laugh. That was all this could be about. I just had to make sure I stayed away.

Fifteen

DOLLY

*A*fter climbing out of Ringer's truck, I waved goodbye and thanked him before heading toward the apartment building. The past four days, Brick had been outside my apartment when I went to bed and woke up. Ringer arrived to take me to work, then brought me back. There had been no more calls or texts from Canyon, but Micah, on the other hand, was calling me at least once, sometimes twice a day.

After the gun incident, when I had freaked out on him, he'd stayed away, but he checked on me. Asked me about my day and listened when I started rambling on about what all had happened. He even laughed and seemed to be enjoying my need to give him more information than he required.

"I'd better stay here." I heard Brick's voice talking to someone at the top of the stairs. "No, I can't do that. Not without Micah's approval. You'll need to call in Tex to help out," he said.

There was no other voice, and I realized he was talking on the phone. I wasn't sure if I should interrupt him or not. I had planned to tell him I was going to see Mrs. Mildred. She hadn't been home the last time I had stopped by to help with her bills, and they were due now. I knew that much.

"Micah claims she's slow. He's not messing with her. Shut that shit down. The boy hasn't even been over here in days," he said in a low voice that I could still hear clear as a bell, seeing as the building was quiet.

I gripped the handrail hard and stood there, letting his words sink in. Slow? What did he mean, Micah said I was slow? I felt bile rise in my throat as my stomach turned.

"She's a sweet girl. Too damn sweet for him. Don't know if she's slow or not, but if Micah wants to think so, it'll keep him from fucking her."

I took a deep breath and let it out slowly, then backed away to stand where I couldn't be seen if he looked down here. Placing a hand on my stomach, I tried to talk myself out of being hurt.

It didn't matter what Micah Abe thought about me. I shouldn't care at all. It had been years since anyone had accused me of having some mental deficiencies. I'd proven them all wrong.

When I didn't hear Brick talking anymore, I waited a few more minutes before walking back to the bottom of the stairs.

If I never laid eyes on Micah Abe again, I would be just fine. The nerve of him to call me slow. What did even know about me? Nothing. He didn't know me enough to have any opinion on my intelligence. He was the slow one.

I called out from the bottom of the stairs, "I'll be up in an hour or so, Brick. I need to help Mrs. Mildred with her bills."

Brick's large body appeared at the top of the stairs. He had a burger in one hand and was chewing. "I'll be right here if you need me," he replied.

I nodded, then headed to the door to the right of the stairs and knocked on Mrs. Mildred's door. The welcome mat needed sweeping off, or maybe I should just replace it. I made a mental note to look at getting her a new one. This one was worn and frayed.

The word *slow* kept taunting me, and I clenched my hands at my sides.

Damn you, Micah Abe.

I had been having a perfectly good day, and he had ruined it. I didn't want to give him that kind of power. Not now or ever.

The door opened, and Mrs. Mildred beamed up at me. "Dolly, I just put on a pot of tea. My great-nephew is here visiting. Come on in and have a cup."

I hadn't met her great-nephew, but I'd heard about him more than once. Mrs. Mildred mentioned him often. She had never had kids. She had two nieces and three great-nieces and one great-nephew. Walen was the only boy. First one in three generations.

"I don't want to intrude. I was just stopping by to help with your bills. I can come back tomorrow," I replied.

She reached out and wrapped her hand around my wrist. "Nonsense! You come right on in and have some tea. Walen was just telling me about his latest rodeo win."

I'd forgotten that she said Walen was a bull rider. It seemed like a dangerous, stupid choice in life, but then I had been dating the vice president of a motorcycle gang. Who was I to judge?

Mrs. Mildred tugged at my arm, and afraid she was going to lose her balance with just one hand on her walker, I went inside the apartment. It smelled of peppermint and licorice, like always.

"I'll just have a cup and then leave you to visit," I told her.

She turned her walker around and started toward the kitchen. "No rush. Come on in and have a seat. I've got a lemon Bundt cake in the oven."

When we walked through the doorway, the man standing over by the coffeepot wasn't tall, but he had wide shoulders and lean hips. His butt looked nice in the jeans he was wearing too. Then, he turned his head, and dark brown eyes locked on me. I hadn't expected Walen the bull rider to be attractive. But he was nice to look at. Firm jawline, covered in a short beard; brown hair cut short; and golden-brown skin from being out in the sun so much, I imagined. What he lacked in height, he made up for with muscle. Thick, corded arms, free of tattoos.

"Walen, honey, this is Dolly Dixon. My neighbor I've told you about. She's come by to help me pay my bills. I told her you just won a pretty penny at the last rodeo. She wants to hear all about it."

That wasn't exactly true, but I wasn't going to correct her.

I forced a smile, feeling slightly embarrassed. "It's nice to meet you, Walen. I tried to tell Mrs. Mildred I'd come back later, but she insisted."

My phone rang, and I pulled it from my pocket to see Micah's name on the screen. I declined it, then stuffed my phone back in my pocket.

He grinned. "She's got a Bundt cake in the oven. We can't eat all of that alone," he replied and motioned to the table. "Please, have a seat. I need your help convincing her to come back to my hotel with me. It's safer than her apartment, and it looks like we have about ten hours before the hurricane hits."

On the ride home from work today, I'd seen people boarding up windows. Even Barnes & Noble had closed early to prep for the storm headed this way. I figured the apartment complex was safe enough, but if we lost electricity or there was an emergency, I liked the idea of Mrs. Mildred being with her great-nephew.

Pulling out a chair, I sat down across from where Mrs. Mildred was sitting.

"No need to worry about a hurricane. I've lived through my share," she said with a wave of her hand. "Walen's one of the best bull riders in the country," she bragged. "What are you ranked now? Fourth, or is it third?"

Walen chuckled and sat down at the end of the table with his coffee. "No, Aunt Mildred. I just broke the top ten last year. I'm still sitting at nine."

She waved a hand as if that didn't matter. "You won almost a hundred grand at that win last month. That ought to put you higher up. How do they determine those rankings?"

Walen looked from his aunt to me. "She's a touch proud," he said to me.

I nodded. "Yes, she is that. I've heard a lot about you."

He groaned and leaned back in the chair. "I'm sorry about that. I can't imagine that is real enjoyable."

"You hush up," Mildred told him. "Dolly likes to hear about it. She said so."

Walen cut his eyes at me with a twinkle in them. He was amused. "I bet," he drawled.

"Walen just broke up with his girlfriend. She wasn't good for him. Didn't appreciate his riding and was bringing him down. It was about time they ended things. It's a shame you started dating that new guy."

My face heated, and I dropped my eyes to the table, not sure how to handle this.

"Aunt Mildred, Lacy was my fiancée, and I'm gonna guess Dolly isn't in need of your matchmaking help either. Why don't we talk, enjoy some of your cake, and not make her any more uncomfortable than she already is?"

Mildred waved a hand at him. "She isn't uncomfortable. Are you, Dolly?"

My eyes widened as I looked from Walen to Mrs. Mildred. "Well, uh—"

"Yes, she is. Why don't you check on the Bundt cake? We don't want it to burn. I'd like to take it with us when we head to the hotel."

"I'm not going to the hotel," she argued.

I jumped up, thankful for the excuse. "I'll do it. You stay put," I told her and hurried over to open the oven.

I needed a reason to leave, but I didn't have a good one, and it was too late to think of one now. It would be clear as day I was running off. I hadn't mentioned needing to prep for the storm when I stopped by. They would know I was lying if I tried using that excuse now. It wasn't in my raising to be rude. Besides, Walen seemed nice enough.

A knock at the door gave me yet another reprieve.

"Cake isn't ready just yet," I told them. "I'll go see who's at the door." Not waiting on Mrs. Mildred to stop me, I left the room, sighing in relief as I reached the front door.

However, once I opened it and found Micah standing there in a pair of black jeans and his bare chest, showing under his open leather vest, I wished I hadn't opened it after all.

"What are you doing here?" I snapped.

He raised an eyebrow. "Looking for you. There's a hurricane headed our way, and I did try to call. You declined it."

Yes, I did. And you called me slow.

"I think everyone is aware of that. I'm fine," I replied.

He shifted his stance and studied me. "You in a snit about something, Tink?"

Yes, Micah Abe, I absolutely am in a snit. Because you called me slow, you jackass.

"Just don't see why you had to stop by my neighbor's, is all."

"Is there a problem, Dolly?" Walen asked from behind me.

Micah's gaze hardened as he looked past me. I was not going to let him make a scene and upset Mrs. Mildred.

"No, Walen. This is my best friend's brother. He's just looking for me. I hate to leave before the cake, but I need to get something for him," I explained.

Walen nodded, not looking sure about my explanation. Right now, Micah looked every ounce the badass biker. His tatted chest was on display, and he had his hair pulled back in a ponytail, but some strands had gotten loose. I was sure Walen was thinking I had myself mixed up with some dangerous folks. He had no idea.

"Yeah, we can wait on you to return. Cake isn't ready yet anyway," he replied. His entire body seemed tense as he kept looking at Micah.

I felt Micah's hand touch my waist, and I almost jumped right out of my skin.

"Let's go." His tone was demanding, and if I wasn't afraid that he'd do something unnecessary, I would tell him to piss off.

Instead, I did my best to hold my smile. "Tell Mrs. Mildred I'll be back when the storm is over to help with the bills."

Walen finally looked at me. He didn't seem pleased with my decision, but he wasn't going to argue with me. "Okay. I'm here until I convince her to leave, if you need me."

"She won't," Micah snarled.

I spun around and glared up at him. "Go," I snapped and shoved past him and out the door.

He closed it, but I didn't stop walking. I stalked toward the stairs, annoyed by the way he had acted toward Walen.

"You sure are moving on from Canyon real damn quick, Tink," he said, entirely too close to me.

I reached the top step and spun around, then tilted my head back to look up at him. Ugh! Why did he have to look like that? So, so panty-droppingly gorgeous. I hated him. I hated him. I had to remember that while looking at his bare chest. Jabbing said chest with my fingernail, I made an angry growl in my throat.

"I went to help Mrs. Mildred pay her bills. That was her great-nephew. He is there to take her with him before the storm hits. That was all that was going on, not that it is your business. You didn't have to be rude."

Micah grabbed my wrist to keep me from the constant jabbing I was doing with my pointed almond-shaped nail. "Sure didn't seem like he was just there for his aunt. He was ready to take me on for you."

"Because you are all biker dude right now with the lack of proper clothin' and messy, windblown hair. He was worried about my safety."

Micah smirked. "No, Tink. He was pissed that I'd come in and messed up his time with you. He'd have asked you out before it was over."

"Go back to the club, Micah. I am just fine without you being here."

Brick cleared his throat, reminding me that he was up here. "Are we good here, or do I need to stay?"

"Go," Micah replied, not looking away from me.

"STAY!" I shouted over him.

A low chuckle from Brick didn't sound very promising that he was gonna side with me.

"It's a fucking miracle you're not married already. You can't go anywhere and not draw a man in," Micah said, surprising me.

I crossed my arms over my chest, not sure if that was meant as an insult or not. "I was visiting my neighbor," I said through clenched teeth.

He smirked then. "So naive."

That was it. I was done with him. Dropping my arms to my sides, I headed for the door. Brick was watching me, but I didn't make eye contact with him. I reached for the door-knob and bit back all the things I wanted to shout at Micah. I wasn't making a scene so that all my neighbors could open their doors and watch.

"I'm not here to fight with you, Tink," Micah said.

Closing my eyes, I took a deep breath. It didn't help. I couldn't stop myself. "Good. Because we both know I'm too slow to keep up!" I replied, jerking the door open and getting inside. Away from him. I didn't want to see his face or listen to his stupid lies about what I had heard him say.

"Fuck," Brick muttered just before the door slammed closed.

I paused at the closed door and listened to see what Micah would say, if he had any explanation.

"What the fuck did you say to her?" Micah demanded.

"I didn't. Jesus, I wouldn't tell her that. I was on the phone, talking to Jars. She must have overheard me. I didn't know she was back."

The door swung back open behind me. Micah was pressed against my back, and his arm went around my front with his palm flat against my stomach. I didn't move. I wished I didn't need to inhale because he smelled really good. And his hard body was warm, leaving no part of my backside untouched by it.

When his breath brushed against my ear, I shivered despite myself.

"I shouldn't have said that." The thickness in his tone made the bones in my body feel as if they had melted. "It was cruel, wrong, and I'm sorry."

The way the last two words had come out fiercely, I believed him. But that didn't change it.

"You're sorry that I heard Brick say it. That I know that's what you think of me," I said just above a whisper.

His hold on me tightened. "Yeah, Tink. I did think that. When you were younger, you were different. But the woman you've become is clearly not slow. I said that before I spent any time around you or talked to you like I have the past few days."

I swallowed against the lump growing in my throat, but said nothing. He wasn't the first person to call me slow. It had just been years since I'd heard it. I'd thought I had over-come that description. That assumption from others. Just because I wasn't outgoing and quick-witted. Just because I didn't have a lot of friends and feel comfortable in a crowd. Just because things triggered my past trauma and I chanted a number in my head—or often out loud. It had made me the weirdo.

"I'm sorry, Tink," he repeated. "I feel like a shit for saying it. I fucking hate that you heard him."

His hand moved on my stomach, slipping under the hem of my shirt. The moment I felt his fingertips on my skin, my pulse quickened. What was he doing?

"I'd never do anything to hurt you. I'd kill anyone who did." His deep voice sounded husky as he brushed his lips across my earlobe. "Tell me you forgive me."

I wasn't sure I could force words out of my mouth. Not with his hand up my shirt, the tip of his thumb brushing awfully close to the underside of my boob, and his heated breath on my ear. My body felt as if a spark had been lit in my stomach and was spreading like a wildfire to all my other parts.

"Please, Tink," he pleaded, then kissed my temple.

I nodded. That was the best I could do, but it was his fault I'd lost all control of my functions.

"Thank you," he said before his hand slid out of my shirt, and the wonderful, overwhelming feeling of his warmth left me.

My own hand flew up to my stomach as I pressed it there in hopes of settling myself.

"Go to your room, Tink." His words sounded like a command. "Pack your things. The storm is threatening to be a Cat 4, and you need to be somewhere safe."

What? How had he switched moods so quickly? He was making my head spin.

"Now," he barked.

I looked back at him, trying to understand what had happened.

"Tink"—his eyes bored into me with a darkness in them I hadn't seen before—"if you don't go to your room, I'm gonna toss your sweet ass on the sofa and fuck you. I came here to get you safe. Now, go."

The spark was back, and this time, it was between my legs. My eyes flew open in surprise. Was he really threatening me with that? Didn't most women beg him for it?

"Don't look at me like that," he warned, taking a step toward me.

I didn't move. Although I was tempted to throw myself at him. I could forget that he'd called me slow. I could forget everything if he would just touch me again. Make me feel like he had before. I'd never had the sensation his words were causing course through me. It was exciting, intoxicating. I wanted more of it.

"You want fucked? Is that it? You want me to jerk that sorry excuse for a skirt up, rip your panties off, and slam my cock inside that needy pussy?"

My knees went weak, and I reached out and grasped for the only thing near me, which happened to be Micah's arm.

Micah grabbed my waist and pushed me back against the wall before placing one palm flat on the space beside my head while his other hand slid between my legs. I let out a gasp as his fingers slid inside my panties.

"Fuck, you're soaked," he groaned.

My face felt like it was on fire while I was panting through the pleasure of being touched there. It was a mix of emotions. I was sure I wasn't supposed to be that wet down there, but the way he was making me feel as he worked his finger inside of me made me not care.

He bowed his head and hissed, "Damn, baby, that's a tight little cunt."

My hips began to work on their own, wanting more of him.

"Keep it up, and you're gonna get fucked hard against this wall. Is that how you like it? Hmm? Does that make you hot, Tink?"

"I don't know," I rasped. I shook my head, wanting more and not getting it.

"Sure you do, baby. Tell me how you want me to take this pussy," he urged before kissing my neck and picking me up until the hard ridge in his jeans pressed between my legs in the exact spot I needed it.

"AH!" I cried out.

"It's a big dick, baby. It's gonna hurt at first. I've never had a cunt that tight. It barely took my finger."

I trembled and rubbed my needy ache against him. "I don't care. It's gonna hurt the first time anyway."

His entire body stilling was the first thing that registered in my lust-hazed mind. The fact he'd completely tensed up was the second. Then, he was gone. I was left panting against the wall, and he had moved away from me several feet.

I stared at him, trying to figure out what I'd said wrong and wanting to throw myself at him and plead for more.

"You're a virgin?" he asked, and the horror in his voice was clear. A bucket of ice being dumped over my head wouldn't have been more effective.

"Yes," I replied.

"FUCK!" he roared, walking past me. He took five long strides, opened the door to my apartment, then walked out, slamming it behind him.

I couldn't move. I stood there, staring at the spot where he had just been standing. Tears filled my eyes as humiliation began to settle over me.

Is that such a bad thing? Yes, it is, Dolly.

Men didn't want unexperienced virgins. It was messy. There was pain and blood. Nothing passionate about that.

Sliding down the wall, I sat on the floor and wrapped my arms around my knees. I would cry. Get it out. Then pull myself together and move on. Forget it and never speak to Micah Abe again.

Sixteen

DOLLY

$\mathscr{I}$ was still on the floor when there was a knock on the door before it slowly opened. Looking up, I saw Brick standing there. His gaze searched the room before it dropped to me. The pity in his eyes was a little more than I could take right now.

"Come on, Dolly. We got to head to the club. It's getting bad out there, and it's just gonna get worse. Don't make this hard, darlin'."

I didn't move. "Why can't I stay here?"

He walked inside the room and knelt down in front of me. "Because the hurricane is a big one. We have a secure place at the club, a generator, and plenty of food. I've been told to get you there even if I have to carry you out, kicking and screaming. And I really don't want to do that."

Sighing, I knew this was a battle I wasn't going to win. The longer Brick had to stay here and convince me, the more danger he was going to be put in when he finally left.

I nodded. "Okay. Let me go pack a bag."

He smiled then and held out a hand for me to take. I let him help me up, then excused myself to go get my things. I wasn't sure how long we would be stuck there. It could be a week or more if it was a Category 4. Electricity would be out everywhere. I couldn't just leave Jeremy here. I knew Mrs. Mildred would be taken care of, and I had been planning on going to see if I could convince Harold to come sleep in my apartment.

Once I was in my room, I grabbed all the essentials and several outfits. Folding them neatly, I worked at a quick pace because I wanted time to help Jeremy and Harold before we went to the club. Grabbing my cell phone off the dresser, I saw where I'd missed a call from Momma and two texts from Pepper.

> Get your ass to the club. NOW!

And...

> I swear to God, if you are not at the club when I get finished prepping the bar for the storm, I am going to be furious.

I typed back.

> Headed there now.

Then, I tucked it in my pocket without calling Mom back. She would be worried, but I didn't have time to reassure her I was going to be safe. I needed to think up a good lie to tell her too.

Brick was standing in the living room with his arms crossed over his chest, staring out the window at the rain and winds that were already here. He glanced back at me. "Ready?"

"I need to check on Jeremy and Harold before we go," I told him.

"Already handled. Jeremy and his dad are gone. They went to a friend of his dad's. Harold is at the Baptist church shelter."

I frowned. "How do you know?"

The corner of his mouth twitched. "Because Micah handled things before he left. He knew you'd want them safe."

I just nodded. What else could I say? He was the most confusing man I had ever known. I wanted to hate him for not wanting me, yet he made it impossible by stepping in when I needed him and handling things for me. Dang him!

"Let's go," Brick said as he walked over to me and took my overnight bag.

I followed him out the door and down to the parking lot.

He stopped at the covering. "You stay here and wait with the bag. I'll go get the truck and pull it up so you don't get wet."

I didn't argue. "Thank you," I said as he took off running into the sideways rain.

My phone began to ring again, and I pulled it from my pocket, expecting to see my mom. Instead, it was a blocked call. I stared at it for a moment more, then hit Decline before shoving it back into my pocket. The only person that could be was Canyon.

Did he think I was slow too? Who else would call me from a blocked number?

Brick pulled his red truck up as close as he could get it and jumped out to run around and help me inside. Once he had my bag and me safely inside, he went back to the driver's side and climbed in. He was soaking wet, and I felt bad about that, but I was also not the one making him do this. Micah was.

"Do you mind getting the towel out of the backseat and handing it to me?" Brick asked.

I unbuckled and turned around to find a beach-sized towel folded up beside where he had put my overnight bag. Grabbing it, I handed it to him, then sat back down and reached for my seat belt again. Brick dried off his arms and face, then ran the towel over his hair before laying it down and finally driving out of the parking lot.

We hadn't gotten far when my phone rang again. Pulling it from my pocket, I saw my mom's name and figured I'd better do this now and get it over with. Hopefully, I could manufacture up a lie that she believed.

"Hey, Momma," I said, mentally preparing for what I would say to her.

"Why haven't you been answering your phone?" she asked. "There is a hurricane about to hit Miami. You'd better be in your car, almost back to Stuart by now. Men from the church came and boarded up the windows, and I got gas for the generator, along with plenty of bread and milk."

She finally stopped long enough to take a breath, and I took it as my cue to start lying.

"Sorry, Momma. I was busy getting myself to safety. I'm not headed home. I just got off work an hour ago. I don't have time to drive there now. The weather here is already deteriorating." My word of the day from my app. I didn't have time to enjoy getting to use it though. I had to finish this before we got to the club. "I'm with Pepper. We are safe and sound. Ready to ride this storm out."

"It's a Cat 4. You don't need to be in Miami. You need to be here in Stuart with me," she said, her voice going high-pitched, the way it did when she was anxious.

"I can't help it, Momma. There is no time to get there. But Pepper's family has a safe place with all that we need to make it through the storm. I am fine. I promise you."

"Please stay inside and don't leave. Call me and update me. Let me know you're okay," she pleaded.

I hated the fear I heard in her voice, but it was time she stopped worrying over me all the time. I was grown now, and she had to let me be an adult. Feeling guilty every time I didn't do what she wanted me to do was my toxic trait.

"I will, Momma. You stay safe, too, and I'll check with you soon. Right now, I need to keep my phone charged though." Okay, that was a bad lie, but I had no other way to get off this call.

"All right. I'm praying. The good Lord will be right there with you."

I seriously doubted the Lord was gonna be anywhere near The Judgment MC compound. "I know, Momma."

"I love you."

"I love you too."

Finally able to end the call, I placed the phone in my lap, relieved that was done. It had been far less dramatic than I had expected. Maybe she was getting better at letting me go.

"You handled her well," Brick said with a smile in his voice.

"Yeah, I'm getting good at lying these days."

He chuckled then. "Sometimes, it's best that our mommas don't know the details. No need in worrying them more than they already do."

I nodded. That I could agree with.

We pulled up to the gate, and it opened moments after I said goodbye to my momma. The parking lot was packed with trucks, SUVs and even some boats.

"Who all is here?" I asked, not seeing a bike anywhere.

"Judgment," he replied. "And their families."

"But there aren't any bikes."

"Those are all stored in the shed out back. No one wants their ride getting trashed," he said, pulling up close to the door. "You run on inside. I'll bring your things."

I started to get out when the door to the club opened and Tex came running out. I watched him as he came straight for me.

"Come on, Dolly," he called out, reaching for me.

I let him help me down, but he picked me up instead and rushed back inside.

I was on my feet in the dark hallway so fast that I had barely gotten wet at all. "Thanks," I said, wiping the little rain that had dampened my arms off with my hands.

"You're welcome."

"Is Pepper here yet?" I asked hopefully.

He shook his head. "No. She is at her bar, boarded in with Anson and Country. It got too bad for them to start this way, and they decided to wait it out there."

Not what I wanted to hear. If I had known that, I would have asked to go to her bar. I'd rather be there than here. Anywhere Micah was not.

Seventeen

MICAH

The text from Brick came through, taking a massive weight off my shoulders.

Here. She's with Nina and Goldie in the kitchen.

I took another pull from the cigarette and tried not to think about the fact that I had caved in and lit one. This was the only thing I could think of to take the edge off. She'd heard me call her slow. That was going to fuck me up for a while. How did I even go about fixing that shit? I'd let my emotions get the better of me. That wasn't me. I didn't let emotions in. So, why was it that little Dolly Dixon was messing me up like this?

I'd hurt her. It was there in her eyes. Yet she had still been ready to let me take her virginity against a damn wall like a caveman. I held my fingers up to my nose and inhaled. Fuck, her scent was still there, and it was sweet. I needed to wash it away, but it was so damn addictive, and I couldn't bring myself to do it. She was a goddamn virgin. I didn't fuck virgins.

Didn't mean I couldn't spread her legs open and feast on that sweet honey though. Listen to her get off with my head between her thighs. Lick her swollen clit and hear her crying out my name.

"FUCK!" I shouted, jamming what was left of my smoke into the ashtray.

I had to stop this. It was Dolly. I couldn't think about Dolly like that. She deserved all the romantic shit. I didn't want anything to do with romantic shit.

Regardless, my desire to go downstairs, snatch her up, haul her to my room, and chain her to my bed was real damn strong. I stuck my middle finger—the one I had slid inside her tight cunt—into my mouth and sucked. I needed to fuck. Problem was, I couldn't bring myself to touch one of the willing cunts here. None of them smelled like this, and they sure as hell didn't taste this good. There was one pussy I wanted, and I couldn't have it.

The door to the library opened, and Brick walked in. I lifted my gaze to meet his as he made his way to the center of the room. I was sitting in Liam's leather chair with my booted feet propped up on his desk. I could see that Brick was pissed at me. Well, join the fucking club. I wasn't real damn happy with me either.

"This place is crawling with Judgment. Some of them that don't understand she's off-limits. You gonna sit up here and ignore that?" Brick asked me.

"You said you left her with Nina and your ol' lady in the kitchen," I replied.

"They're not gonna be there all damn night with her, and the way some of these horny-ass prospects are, I don't want that shit on Goldie's shoulders. You had me bring her here. Now, it's your turn to take care of her."

I dropped my feet to the floor and stood up. He was right, but that didn't mean I wanted to listen to it. "You think me taking care of her makes her safer?" I asked. "I almost fucked her earlier. She's a virgin. I can't be near her."

A low, deep chuckle came from Brick, and I glared at him. "You're afraid to fuck her."

"Yeah, because virgins are clingy. They get attached. They expect things."

"Is that what you're telling yourself?" he asked, grinning. "Because the way I see it, you don't want to fuck her because you won't be able to stop. You will want to keep her, and no woman has ever held that power over you." He paused. "Not even Calista. When she left, you didn't even chase her."

Calista had been the only girl I'd ever loved. But that had been years ago. I started to argue, but stopped. Was he right? Was I scared I wouldn't be able to get enough? That I'd keep wanting more?

"She's a sweet girl. Too damn nice for the likes of your ass. But seeing as she looks at you like you hung the goddamn moon, I can't say it's a bad thing. She wants you. You want her. Just get this over and fuck. If she owns you after that, then so be it.. You've been a fucking whore for long enough."

"Shut up," I growled, stalking past him.

I wasn't going to stand here and listen to this. I was going to get weak and give in. I needed to go wash her smell from my fingers. Get this out of my head. Stop fantasizing about it.

"It's not a prison sentence. First taste I got of Goldie's pussy, and I was done. Happily so. I didn't want another one. She had all I needed with her pot of gold."

I didn't look back at him. He was one of the few happily married men I knew. Men weren't meant to be tied down to one woman. It was their downfall. It messed them up. Took away their youth. I wasn't falling into that trap.

I jerked open the door and got away from Brick and all his words that were digging into my skull and trying to settle in and stay. Telling me that just maybe I could have her. That it would be worth it. That I wouldn't end up breaking her heart. I'd already hurt her once, and the idea of doing it again nearly brought me to my knees. I couldn't stand it.

Getting her out of my head was what I needed to do. I'd go get one of the girls and fuck her until Dolly's sweet scent was gone. If I didn't, then there was a good chance I'd snap and lock Dolly in my bedroom and keep her naked in my bed all damn night.

Eighteen

DOLLY

The pink cocktail that Goldie had given me tasted nothing like vodka. It was fruity with a slight kick to it. If I had to stay down here with these loud, rough, slightly scary people, then I needed something to ease my nerves. Two men had already gotten in a fight. Brick and Tex had broken it up. There was a blonde woman who was currently straddling a guy I didn't know on one of the sofas, and I was afraid to look in that direction again because I wasn't so sure they weren't having sex.

"Hey, beautiful," a guy I didn't know said as he leaned against the bar, facing me.

I looked up at him and forced a smile. He was around my age, maybe a year or so older. His arms were bare and covered in tattoos, and he was lean but still built well.

"Off-limits, Pinch," Nina informed him. "Go flirt with one of the club sluts."

The guy grinned at Nina, but his gaze came right back to me. "Why would I want to do that when there's a pretty thing like this one sitting here, all alone?"

"Unless you want Micah on your ass, you will walk away," Nina warned.

He didn't budge, but his grin grew bigger. "Micah's busy fucking Dylan," he replied. Then, he leaned closer to me. "Tell me, sweetheart, what's your name?"

I'd never been hit in the chest, but I imagined that the current sensation that slammed into me at his words was what it would feel like. My nails bit into my thigh as I squeezed, trying to control the raw emotion creeping through me.

I wasn't enough. I was never enough. I would never be enough. No one wanted me. I was nothing more than a pawn to the only guy who I'd thought wanted me. How much more rejection could I take before I cracked completely?

"PINCH!"

Micah's shout caused me to jump, startled. The room quieted, and the guy in front of me paled as he began moving back from me, his eyes widening. The sting from my nails breaking my skin didn't concern me. It was a relief in a way. The pain taking away from the reality of how unwanted I was. Reminding me of how I had once used that like a drug. I'd forgotten how it felt, how it numbed the truth.

"Don't look at her again." Micah's voice was threatening. "Don't talk to her. Don't breathe her fucking air."

"About time you got down here," Goldie said to Micah with a scowl on her face.

Micah was beside me, his body close enough that his arm brushed against my back. "You okay?" he asked, leaning down toward me.

One hundred twenty-two, one hundred twenty-two, one hundred twenty-two.

"Dolly?" His voice sounded concerned.

I had to respond.

One hundred twenty-two, one hundred twenty-two, one hundred twenty-two.

I managed to nod my head. The guy he'd called Pinch muttered an apology in my general direction, then headed to the other side of the room.

Micah's fingers wrapped around my upper arm. "Come with me." His words didn't leave anything up for discussion.

He was gently pulling me from my seat. I could either fight him or stand up. Not wanting to draw more attention to myself, I did as told, although I hoped he intended to take me to a room and leave me. Talking to him after what had happened at the apartment earlier would be more humiliation dropped on top of what I was already suffering.

I could feel everyone's eyes on me. I kept my gaze down, not enjoying being the center of attention. I was unfamiliar with it, and I was finding I didn't care for it at all. Micah wrapped an arm around my shoulders and led me out of there, through the red door. Once we were in the dark hallway and away from prying eyes, I moved away, shrugging him off me.

One hundred twenty-two, one hundred twenty-two, one hundred twenty-two.

"I prefer you not touch me," I said, walking away from him. Unsure where it was I should be going.

"We both know that's not true, Tink," he said behind me.

I stopped and inhaled a deep breath. I wouldn't allow this to break me. I was stronger than that. I had to be. I'd lived through worse.

"Just take me to a room and drop me off. I want to be alone and get through this hell so that I can go back home," I replied.

Micah walked past me and toward the stairs. "Fine," was all he said.

I fell into step behind him and tried to tamp down all the anger, hurt, and mix of several emotions churning in my chest. I should add *hate* to that list. I hated that he could make me feel like this. That I cared what he thought of me. I *hated* that I wanted his approval. And I hated that he'd pushed me to self-harm. It had been years since I'd injured myself on purpose. To deal with my inner turmoil. I'd been to therapy for it. I had overcome it. Yet Micah had sent me back to it with little work on his part at all.

We reached the top, and he turned right, but he didn't stop at the door to the room I had been left in the last time I was here. Instead, he kept walking until he reached the end of the hallway and opened the last door, then stood back and motioned for me to go inside. I didn't bother looking at him as I walked by him and into the new room.

I was so focused on showing no reaction to him at all that I didn't realize the room looked like it belonged to someone. It was clearly lived in. The door slammed, startling me. I spun around to see Micah standing there, watching me.

"Where are we?" I asked.

"My room."

His room? My eyes scanned the area again, paying more attention to details. The king-size bed didn't take up even half the space. The room was twice the size, if not three times bigger, than the other room I had seen. A massive flat screen covered the wall across from the bed. A black dresser sat below it. There was a guitar in a stand in the left corner of the room, a pair of jeans thrown over a brown leather chair. And the scent, it was as if I had shoved my face in Micah's chest.

"Why did you bring me here?" I asked him, finally turning my gaze back to his.

"All the rooms are full. My bed is the only available one," he replied, then began to shrug off his leather vest as he made his way over to the dresser. "It's a big bed, Tink. You'll have plenty of room."

Was he being serious? He was planning on us both sleeping in the same bed? My hands fisted at my sides. Did he think this was funny?

"I won't sleep in that bed," I said, staring at it with loathing. Knowing what he'd been doing up here just a few minutes ago.

He cocked an eyebrow at me. "Is that so? Interesting since you were ready to let me fuck you just a few hours ago."

The humiliation from his words hit me, and I closed my eyes and tried to focus on not showing any emotion. When I looked at him again, I felt all the anger, rejection, and betrayal rise up inside me.

"I had a moment of insanity," I snapped. "Let's blame it on my being…slow."

Micah took three long strides until he was standing so close that I could feel the heat from his body.

"Don't ever," he said through clenched teeth, "say shit like that about yourself again."

I tilted back my head and glared up at him. "I'm sorry. I was unaware only you were allowed to insult and demean me."

His nostrils flared as he stared down at me. The flash of regret I saw in his pale blue eyes wasn't enough for me to feel any sympathy for him.

"Dolly, I…" His gaze dropped then, and his entire body tensed. "What the fuck happened to your leg?" he demanded angrily, then went down on one knee and pushed my skirt up further to see the smeared blood from where my nails had broken my skin. "Who did this?!" The threat in his voice made me shiver. But his touch probably also had something to do with that.

"I did," I bit out, pulling my leg free from his hold as I stepped back.

He stayed there on the floor, staring at me as if he didn't know me. Confusion softened his expression, but his jawline told me he was still clenching his teeth. "You did this? On purpose?"

I didn't have to answer him. He deserved nothing from me. Yet it seemed impossible to say nothing when he was looking at me like that. As if he was physically in pain himself.

"I didn't mean to. I was dealing, internally. It happened," I explained, then turned around so he couldn't see my face or the damage I had done to my thigh. "Just leave me alone. Please. I just want to be alone." So I could curl up and cry without an audience.

I heard his footsteps on the hardwood floor, but he wasn't leaving. I closed my eyes just as his hands wrapped around my upper arms.

"I don't want to leave. I want to be here. With you."

No, no, no. He would not do this to me. I couldn't ride the roller coaster of emotions that Micah Abe could send me spiraling on and come out intact.

"You made it very clear you didn't want me."

His grip on my arms tightened. "You think my leaving was not wanting you?" He let out a sigh. "Tink, that was the opposite. That was me saving you from me. You deserve better."

Of course he'd make himself out to be the hero. Soften the blow so I wouldn't hate him. Micah was an expert at manipulating women and men alike.

"I'm sure that was the reason you stared at me as if I were a freak of nature, then bolted from the room," I replied and tried to free myself from his grasp. My attempt was done in vain.

Micah pulled me back against his chest with ease, as if I hadn't been pulling in the opposite direction. "Nothing," he whispered, his mouth close to my ear, "about you is a freak of nature." His right hand slid up and over my shoulder, then brushed my hair back. His thumb began to caress my neck in a small, circular movement. "You're beautiful, sweet, thoughtful, kind, charming. I can't think of a man that is good enough for you. That deserves to have the privilege to touch you." His lips pressed against my temple. "I sure as fuck don't. But I want to. So bad that it's eating me alive inside. The smell of you on my fingers is driving me crazy. I've almost sucked your taste completely off, trying to get more of it."

My body rebelled against my brain as it trembled and seemed to melt back against his hard chest. His words held power over my good sense.

"Sit down on the bed and let me get something to clean up your leg. I don't like seeing you hurt," he said as his hands moved to my waist, and he moved me forward until I had no choice but to turn and sit down, like he had instructed.

My eyes slowly traveled up his jean-clad thighs and stopped at the bulge in his crotch. Surprised, I snapped my eyes up to his face. I felt my own cheeks heating as a devilish grin tugged at his lips.

"Stay here," he said simply, then made his way to the bathroom door that stood open on the other side of his room.

When he was out of sight, I dropped my focus to my thigh.

The marks from my nails were clearly visible, even with the smeared blood surrounding them. Shame began to unfurl in my chest. It had been years since I had taken a knife to myself. Once, it had been a need so strong that I couldn't control it. Memories of locking myself in the attic with my dad's pocketknife haunted me.

"Tell me why." Micah's urge wasn't harsh, but it felt as if it was a demand. He knelt down in front of me again and took a damp cloth to wipe away the blood. He looked up at me once he had it clean. "Your nails?"

I nodded, but as to telling him the why, I wasn't ready for that yet. The why was a part of my past that only Pepper knew about.

He ran the pad of his thumb just under the broken flesh. I wanted to cover it up, hide it. Especially from him. It revealed too much. More than I was capable of sharing. Micah wasn't someone that others ignored. He always got what he wanted. But this wasn't something I could give him. The reason why was mine. It had to stay there, locked away. I feared talking about it would bring it back. The dark draw to cause pain that had once held me.

"This might sting a little," he warned me as he took the antibiotic ointment and squeezed some on his fingertip, then coated the marks I'd left.

The coating didn't hurt, but there was a warm tingling with it that I couldn't be sure was the cream or just my body's reaction to Micah's touch.

He cleaned the excess from his finger, then opened a bandage and placed it over my wounds. He took my hand and found the blood under my fingernails, then cleaned it with the cloth. Once he was done, I expected him to stand up, but instead, he bent his head and kissed right below the bandage, then lifted his gaze to mine.

"Never hurt any part of this beautiful body again," he told me with a fierceness in his expression. "If you need to hurt something, then hurt me. Not you. Never you."

I'd never hurt another person in my life, but his request—or rather demand—felt as if he had managed to reach inside me where I was the most damaged and soothe it, the way he had my visible marks. My head knew that allowing Micah to have any hold on me was asking for future agony, but the rest of me wanted nothing more but to beg him to hold me. Even if for a moment. It was foolish, but he made me feel safe. I'd had very little of that in my life.

"These heels you wear are sexy as hell, but they can't be comfortable." His tone was softer, slightly teasing. He slipped my shoes off my feet and ran his hand over them, massaging the ache before letting them go.

When he began to stand back up, I knew it was over. I'd be alone again, and the torment of the past would seep in. I'd handle it the best way I could and hope that my will was stronger than my urge.

He nodded his head toward the other end of the bed. "Get up there and lie down. I swear the sheets are clean. No one has been in them but me."

Sinking into his scent might be the worst idea for my current mental state, but I wanted it. If I had to be left with my demons to battle, then at least I could pull the covers over me and soak in where his body had been. I was done arguing or trying to save myself from the future misery this would bring me. I scooted back and pulled down the blankets to slide underneath. The soft warmth gave me little comfort, but it was better than nothing.

Micah bent down and began to unlace his boots. I watched him in silence, unsure what to make of it. When he stood back up and made his way over to the bed, hope slowly began to unfurl inside my chest. He pulled back the covers, and still wearing his jeans, he slid in beside me.

"Roll over," he said in a husky whisper.

I was facing him, and I wanted to keep looking at him, but I did as he had asked. Once I was turned, his arm came around me, and he pulled me back until I was pressed against his chest.

"You're staying with me?" I asked, surprised and almost giddy at the thought of being held like this by Micah Abe.

"Seems there is no place else I'd rather be," he replied. He pressed his face into my hair, then inhaled deeply. "Go to sleep, Tink. I'll be here."

Nineteen

MICAH

I didn't normally drink before noon, but I'd barely slept. The deep-seated need to punish someone had slowly built inside me until I felt as if I was going to explode. The only thing that had kept me sane was holding Dolly. Her body tucked against me, safe where no one could hurt her.

"What? It's too damn early for phone calls," Pepper grumbled into the phone as I gripped the glass of whiskey in my hand, glaring at shelves of books in front of me.

"Tell me why Dolly would hurt herself," I demanded, knowing that if anyone knew the answer to what had happened last night, it would be my sister.

She'd known Dolly since they had been seven years old. All I knew of her was the little girl who would come over to play when I was visiting. I realized last night that I was clueless to her past. I knew she had a momma who was overprotective, but that was it.

"Shit." Pepper's muttered curse made my chest tighten. "What did she do?" she asked.

The anxiousness in her tone wasn't lost on me. She knew. She was worried.

"Dug her nails so fucking deep into her thigh that she's gonna have scars. She bled, Pepper. And she didn't even wince when I cleaned it. She seemed almost numb."

And it was fucked up. Something in her eyes last night had hit me so deep that it was hard to control myself. I'd wanted to go destroy whatever it was that had caused this. I hated seeing the misery in her amber depths. Dolly was all that was good in this world, and knowing there was something that dark that had gotten to her once enraged me.

"Where is she now?" Pepper asked.

"In my bed."

"WHAT?! Please tell me that is a fucking joke. I swear to God, Micah, I will cut off your damn dick if you fucked her. I trusted you—"

"Calm down. I didn't fuck her. I held her. She was…she was broken. I can't…" I stopped, unable to explain to my sister just how unstable I felt, seeing her like that. It was more than she or anyone needed to know.

Pepper let out a long, relieved sigh. "That's probably going to be an issue, too, but not as devastating," she said. "I'm getting dressed and heading over there if I can. I don't know what the roads look like yet. Have you seen the news?"

I hadn't done anything but remove myself from the bed before my raging hard-on scared the shit out of Dolly. Then, I'd come in the library to drink.

"Tell me what happened to her."

I didn't need Pepper coming to the rescue, and I sure as hell wasn't going to allow her to take Dolly from me. She was staying her ass in my room. Under my protection.

"I can't. It's…it's not my story to tell," Pepper replied. "Just please, Micah, don't mess with her head. This bullshit with Canyon clearly affected her more than she let on. I should have known. She's a pro at hiding her shit and internalizing her pain."

Fury rolled through me as I slammed the glass in my hand onto the table. "This is because of Canyon?"

"What else could it be? Dolly has come a long way. She's overcome so much, and I let myself believe that the past was finally behind her. Canyon has messed with her head, and she isn't strong enough to deal with that."

I was going to kill him.

"The roads aren't safe yet. Stay there. I'll take care of Dolly."

"Micah, you have no idea what—"

"I will take care of Dolly. I don't need to know what happened in the past to take care of her."

"Micah—"

I ended the call before my sister could say one more word about fucking Canyon Acree. I'd never hated anyone more than I did that man right now. If he came near Dolly again, I would need Blaise Hughes's pull to keep me out of prison.

I stalked toward the door. I was going back to my room. Back to Tink. Leaving her there in my bed, curled up and alone, had been painful, but I'd needed to know why last night had happened. If I wasn't going to know the why, then I was going to be the one to stop it. I wasn't sure I could breathe normally again until I knew my Tink was happy and secure.

Tex was leaving his room and headed for the stairs when I walked back into the hallway.

"Tree is down right outside the gate. We're heading out to cut it up and remove it. You coming?" he asked as I walked past him without a glance.

"No," I snapped as the clawing urgency to get back to Dolly grew stronger.

"I see. Well, all right then," Tex drawled behind me.

He didn't see shit, but I wasn't going to explain myself to him or anyone. I didn't even fucking understand me right now anyway. How could anyone else?

Jerking my door back open, I walked inside to see Dolly still sleeping in the middle of my bed. The sight eased me some, but not completely. There was still that unknown monster I had to slay for her. I just needed to be pointed in the right direction, and I'd fix it. She would never be tormented by it again.

The door clicked shut, and I locked it, then went to the bed to climb back in beside her. Holding her would help. I just needed her back against me again.

She began to turn as I slid under the covers. I watched as she blinked several times while she stared at my neck and chest. A grin tugged at my lips. Damn, she was sweet.

"Morning," I said, drawing those pretty eyes up to mine.

She studied me for a moment, and then a small smile touched her lips. "Good morning."

The sleepy thickness in her voice made my dick twitch. The desire to spread her legs and bury my face between them was almost impossible to resist. Knowing she had a darkness haunting her, defeating her, and she was fragile were the only things keeping me from giving in to my lust.

"Did you sleep well?" she asked me.

"Yeah," I lied.

I watched as she pulled her bottom lip between her teeth and chewed on it nervously. Did she know how enticing that was? That mouth of hers had been teasing me since I'd walked into the bar and found her with Canyon. Jesus Christ, she had to stop that.

I reached over and pulled her plump lip free, then brushed my thumb over it, wishing I could taste it. Lick it. Suck on it. "That's a little more than I can handle, Tink."

A frown puckered her brow. "What?"

God, she was innocent. She had no clue the tempting little package she was.

"Biting your lip, sweetheart. You've got the perfect mouth, and that only makes me think about all the things I'd like to do to it."

Her eyes widened, and she sucked in a quick breath. I let her mind work through my words and enjoyed seeing the different emotions that flashed across her face as she did so.

"What..." She started, then paused and swallowed. "What do you want to do to it?" The slight quaver in her voice just about broke me.

It had taken a lot for her to ask me that. She wasn't the kind of girl who teased men or used her power over them to get what she wanted. She had no fucking clue she had any power.

I slid my hand to cup the side of her face. I should get up. Stop this before I couldn't. I should do a lot of things, but I wasn't getting out of this bed. There was no point in telling myself it was the right thing to do. I wasn't that strong.

Leaning down, I brushed my lips against hers and moved my hand down to her neck until my thumb was over the pulse there. The quickening of it made me feel like a damn king. I ran the tip of my tongue over the swollen bottom lip just as she opened for me. Taking full advantage of the invitation, I managed to tamp down my desire to climb on top of her and crush my mouth against hers.

Instead, I savored her. The purity of her uncertainty was going to drive me wilder than any kinky shit I'd experienced in the past. This was another level of longing. It exceeded anything else. A shudder ran through her body, and she pressed closer to me, sliding her fingers into my hair. This wasn't going to be enough for me. I'd opened Pandora's box, and I was going to either own it or destroy it. The frenzy building in my chest wasn't keeping me sane enough to make the right decision.

The moan from Dolly snatched away the last string of my self-control. I tore my mouth from hers, and I made my way down her throat, needing to taste all of her. Every fucking inch. When I reached the collar of her shirt, I took the unwanted fabric and pulled it up, needing it off her. Hating any barrier that was in my way. She lifted her arms, allowing me to easily discard it. Pausing, I took a moment to memorize the sight of the lacy pale pink bra covering her tits before getting it off her. With each panting breath she took, her chest bounced gently, making it hard for me to remain focused on my goal. Lowering my head, I pulled one of her hardened nipples into my mouth and sucked.

"Oh!" she cried out as her hand went to the back of my head and held me there.

I couldn't remember the last woman I'd been with who I took the time to do this to, but Dolly's pleasure had me giving each breast my undivided attention.

When I finally began to travel down her stomach, she let go of my head, and her hands fisted the sheet beneath us. Smiling up at her, I unbuttoned her skirt before tugging it down while leaving the matching pink panties on. I needed some barrier, no matter how flimsy, to keep from sinking my dick into her like a madman.

Tossing her skirt to the floor with the rest of her discarded clothing, I took her legs and draped them over my shoulders. Taking only a moment to appreciate the view, I inhaled that addictive scent that had almost been my undoing yesterday. The honeyed delirium that met my tongue snapped any and all restraint I had left. The reasons why I had to stop this didn't matter.

"Micah! Oh God," she gasped, digging her heels into my back as she clawed frantically at the bed.

The power of seeing perfection come apart while I ate the most luscious pussy I'd ever tasted ranked as the best moment of my life.

Using my hand, I opened her folds and lapped at the sweetest cream I'd ever had. Her body bucked as she cried out my name.

"Come on my tongue, baby," I urged her, wanting more of it.

"Oh my God," she moaned as she grabbed a handful of my hair and pulled. "OH MY GOD!"

A shudder racked her body as I inhaled her release, and she began to ride my face. It made me want to pound my chest. I'd done this. I had given her this nirvana. Me. Not Canyon.

At the thought of the other man, my body tensed. I felt as if a vise had clamped around my throat, and my chest felt like it was going to explode. I fought back the roar building inside me and tore myself away from her, only to remove my jeans and underwear while watching her naked body spread out for me, panting as she came down from the high I had given her.

I reached for the drawer in the bedside table and took out a condom. Her eyes followed me as I tore it open and rolled it down my hard dick. This wasn't what I had intended to do. She was untouched. I didn't deserve this, but I would be damned if another man had her. No one else deserved her either. There would never be anyone good enough for her. At least I knew with me, she would be worshipped properly.

I stared down at her as I knelt between her legs. I didn't want to give her time to stop this, but I also knew I couldn't take her virginity without knowing she was giving it to me willingly. I could hear my own heavy breathing as I waited. It took self-control I hadn't known I possessed not to bury myself inside her.

"Micah," she said, and the question in her eyes was echoed in that one word.

"Do you want this?" I asked in a hoarse whisper.

If she said no, I might not ever recover.

"Yes, please." Her voice was so soft that I almost didn't hear her over the pounding of my heart. But the *please* had humbled me to the point that I struggled to inhale my next breath.

I wasn't worthy of this, but by God, I would make it special. Lowering myself over her, I trailed kisses from her breasts, along her collarbone, to the pulse in her neck, up to her mouth that was slightly open.

"I'll do everything I can to ease the pain," I promised her.

"I don't care about the pain. I just want it to be you."

Closing my eyes for a moment, I took a deep breath, then let it out. "You say shit like that, and it makes it hard to go slow."

She reached up and cupped the side of my face with her small hand. "Then, don't. I want it to be good for you too."

A low chuckle rumbled in my chest. "Tink, I can promise you, that is not gonna be a problem."

I placed a kiss on her lips as I pressed against her entrance. She tensed beneath me as I began to ease inside her.

"Relax, baby," I urged her as I bent my head over the crook of her neck and did my best to do this slowly.

She nodded, opening her legs wider as her breathing deepened. I sank deeper until I felt the barrier. This was a first. Knowing about the hymen and actually encountering one was two different things.

I had never fucked a virgin. I'd heard enough talk to know that it hurt them, they bled, and it wasn't good for the female. I'd be damned if that was how it was going to be for Dolly. She would enjoy this. I'd make sure the pleasure outweighed the bad. If I could keep from fucking coming too soon. The way she was squeezing my dick was the closest thing to heaven I would ever get. I'd bet my life this was better than the fucking pearly gates.

"It's okay," she whispered, then kissed my neck.

I thrust into her at those words and stilled as she let out a cry and clung to me. My dick was buried inside her completely now, and every muscle in my body was locked up as I clenched my teeth and fought the desire to get more of this. Feel her tight cunt as I pumped in and out of her.

She lifted her hips then and hissed through her teeth. I managed to not start fucking her like an animal as she slid her legs up mine and let out a low moan. Jesus H. Christ, I deserved an award for this.

"Please," she begged.

I didn't know if she was asking me to move or to get out. She ran her hands down my back until her nails bit into my asscheeks. I was going to take that to mean that she wanted me to stay. Easing back, I began to gently pump in and out of her. Each time going a little deeper, pushing a little harder. Bringing myself closer and closer to my release.

"Micah," she breathed as she grabbed my biceps. "Micah!"

Her inner walls clamped down hard on my cock, and I felt the tremor as it rolled through her body.

FUCK YES! She was coming.

"That's it, baby. Come for me," I panted.

"OH GOD!" she cried out and began to jerk as she clung to me.

It was then I felt it. The rush of fluid hitting my balls and the inside of my thighs. Fucking hell! She was squirting.

Any restraint I had left was gone.

"FUCK! I want to fill that pussy up," I groaned as I lost control of my own body and began pounding into her.

I'd give anything to rip the damn condom off and unload inside her. I wanted her to squirt on me raw. Sweet little virgin was going to own me, and I didn't give a damn.

"AH!"

Her small yelp only drove me further.

My body jerked against her as I shouted her name. The pulse from my release caused me to tremble with each shot of cum that filled the fucking condom. By the time I finally stopped, I was lightheaded. I rolled to the side, not wanting to crush her with my weight, but pulled her body with me, not willing to break the connection yet. I wanted to stay inside of her longer.

With a shuddered breath, I opened my eyes and looked at her. She was smiling at me. A pleased look in her eyes made me grin back at her. I should be asking her if she was okay and cleaning her up, but fuck that. I wanted her like this for as long as I could have her. Once we left this bed, reality would set in. What I had done would have to be dealt with. Everything would change.

"You gonna just keep smiling at me all pretty and sweet or say something?" I teased.

She ducked her head and laughed. "What do I say?"

I reached over and tucked her hair behind her ear. "Oh, I don't know. You can tell me what a god I am and praise my skills."

She lifted her head and looked back up at me with amusement dancing in her eyes. "Hmm...a god, huh?"

I nodded. "I not only gave you an orgasm your first time, but I also made you squirt."

She licked her bottom lip and suddenly looked unsure. "That...was that what I did? I wasn't sure, and I felt it, but..."

Unable to stop myself, I leaned down and kissed her lips. "Yeah, that's what you did. And if I hurt you after, that's not completely my fault. That tight little pussy squirting on me was more than I could take. I lost my control after that."

She blushed then and shut her eyes tightly. I kissed her and started to deepen it when banging on the door interrupted me.

"OPEN THIS DOOR, MICAH, OR I WILL BREAK IT DOWN!" Pepper screamed from the other side.

Shit.

II

"When love is not madness, it is not love."
—Pedro Calderon de la Barca

Twenty

DOLLY

Micah jumped out of bed as if he couldn't get away from me fast enough. I grabbed the covers and pulled them up to my neck as he began to take off the condom.

"Give me a minute," he called out to Pepper.

Why was she here? And what was she going to do when she found me in here with him? I watched, unsure of what to do, and waited for Micah to tell me something. He reached for his jeans and pulled them on.

"Dolly? Are you in there! Micah, I am going to kill you!" Pepper yelled.

I was verging on panicking when Micah looked at me and then glared at the door.

"Fuck," he muttered. He grabbed one of his T-shirts and tossed it to me. "Put this on and…go on into the bathroom. Get a shower. I will deal with her psychotic ass."

More banging. "MICAH, OPEN NOW!"

I scrambled to get the shirt on, then hurried off the bed and into the bathroom. Micah's gaze followed me, but I was afraid to look him in the eye. Was he mad at me? Surely not. But then what if Pepper was mad at me and him and that made him mad at me?

Closing the door, I locked it, then leaned back against it and stared at my reflection in the mirror. Did I look different? I felt different. At least my body did. There was an ache between my legs and a slight sting. I lifted the shirt to see how bloody it looked down there, but jumped, dropping it at the sound of Pepper shouting at Micah.

"WHERE IS SHE?! YOU! YOU! I can't believe you did this! It didn't even take a week! Did you stick her in the bathroom? Seriously?"

"Pep, calm the fuck down," Micah told her.

"Don't *Pep* me and do not tell me to calm down. That is my best friend you're hiding in the bathroom after you…" She stopped, and I heard footsteps followed by a, "DAMMIT, MICAH!"

"It isn't what you think," he said.

"That's blood on your sheets, and MY best friend is in your bathroom. Yeah, Micah, it is what I think."

"No, it's not. At least not exactly. Could you just go downstairs and get something to drink or eat? We will be down shortly."

"And leave her up here with you?" she shot back at him.

"Why not? What else is there for me to do to her?"

I tensed at his words, and a sick knot formed in my stomach.

"You are a bastard—you know that? She deserved more than…than you."

"You think I don't know that?"

"Then, why did you do it?" Pepper hissed angrily.

"Because…fuck. I don't know. I just did."

Closing my eyes, I inhaled slowly, willing myself not to cry. I had basically begged him to. It wasn't like having sex with me was going to make him fall in love with me. We barely knew each other. He was my best friend's older brother I had once been obsessed with, and I was…I was me. I was not going to get emotional and weepy because I didn't have some magic vagina to make him want me for something more.

"I will never, never forgive you for this. Just…let her get cleaned up, and I'll take her home. The roads are cleared enough," Pepper said.

I listened to her footsteps fade away and the sound of the door closing behind her. I waited for Micah to come this way, but I heard nothing.

With a heaviness in my chest, I walked over and turned on the shower, waited for it to get warm, and stepped under the spray of the water. Washing off every place he had kissed me, touched me. The pink tint to the water as it went down the drain caused my vision to blur, and for a moment, I allowed myself a few tears.

Not because I had lost my virginity. Good riddance.

I cried because I had thought that it meant more to Micah…that I meant something to him. But I had just been another girl in his bed. I was as interchangeable as the others. It was my own stupidity. I should have enjoyed the experience and not opened my heart up to him.

My fingers brushed over the bandage on my leg he'd put there, and I let the memory of how gentle he'd been seep in before I could stop it. Taking the edge of the Band-Aid, I ripped it off. The red marks were scabbed over. I bunched up the bandage in my fist and tilted my head back as the water washed away my tears.

Finishing my shower, I got out and dried off. My eyes weren't puffy, and it didn't look as if I had been crying. Satisfied with that, I wrapped the towel around me and opened the bathroom door, ready to face Micah. Only he wasn't there. His sheets were also gone. On his mattress, my clothes were spread out neatly, and my heels sat beside them. It was just one more slap in the face. I wasn't even worthy of him sticking around to talk to me before I left.

I dressed, ran my fingers through my damp hair, found my phone, and headed out the door. I was ready to go home. Even if that meant facing Pepper.

Just as I made it to the stairs, a blonde blocked my way. She sneered at me as if I was something distasteful. I hadn't met her before, but it seemed like she knew who I was.

"So, you're the boring little virgin who didn't meet up to Micah's expectations," she said, then smirked. "I'll make sure to meet his needs for him. I always do."

"Dylan, shut your trap and leave the girl alone," Tex called out from the now-open library door.

She glanced down the hall at him, then back at me. "Bye-bye," she replied, then brushed past me.

I watched as she walked in the direction of the library. The cutoff jeans she was wearing left part of her bottom hanging out. I hated her.

Needing to get away from this place, I hurried down the stairs. Pepper was standing there with her arms crossed over her chest. When she saw me, I could see the concern in her eyes, and when she opened her arms to me, I rushed into them.

"Let's go," she said. "I called your landlord, and the electricity is on there."

I nodded, but I didn't trust myself to talk.

Pepper threaded her fingers through mine and held my hand all the way down the dark hallway and into the parking lot. She opened the passenger side of her Mustang and waited for me to climb in, then closed the door behind me before making her way to the other side.

When she was inside the car, she buckled, then looked at me. "He's my brother, and I love him, but it will be a long time before I can look at him again. He's a bastard, and I am so sorry. I should have come here last night. I trusted him, and I shouldn't have."

I reached over and took her hand. "Stop. He didn't rape me. I asked for it. He did what I'd asked. And…and it was good. Better than good. It was amazing."

The pain in her eyes made her thoughts on the matter clear. "You understand that sex is just sex to Micah? Nothing more. It holds no meaning or emotion to him."

I nodded. I knew that. Now.

She sighed heavily. "One day, the right guy will come along. With him, it will be everything you deserve."

I looked out the window as she drove off The Judgment's property. "Or maybe I'm better off alone."

"Don't say that."

I turned my attention to her. "Why? You seem fine alone. You haven't dated in two years. Do you think the right guy is going to come along for you one day?"

She laughed and shook her head. "I am not like you. I don't want a man. You…you're softer. Kinder. You crave that connection. Even if you don't want to admit it. You are the perfect female. I am the exact opposite."

I frowned. She always said I didn't see myself clearly, but *she* didn't see herself the way the rest of the world did. Men paused to watch her walk by. When she walked into a room, it began to revolve around her without her realizing it. I'd tried to tell her that in the past, but she never listened.

Pepper reached across and grabbed my hand. "Talk to me about last night. Why did you hurt yourself?" Her eyes dropped to the marks on my leg before she looked back at the road.

"I don't know," I lied, not wanting to talk about it.

"Dolly, if you need to see a psychologist again, then I'm sure—"

"No. I'm fine. It was nothing. Just drop it."

"I can't drop it if you are hurting. We both know what happens if you try and internalize. I am your friend. You can trust me. You know that."

I nodded and hated that my eyes were burning. "It is over. It won't happen again. I swear."

Twenty-One

MICAH

"arnes & Noble opened back up, and so has the library. Dolly is going back to work. I'm heading to the bar, and I doubt I can stay tonight. Send someone over here, but so help me GOD, it'd better not be you." Pepper's heated tone came through on the line.

I took one more pull from the cigarette in my hand, then dropped it to the pavement and covered it with my boot. My eyes were locked on the apartment window across the street. Pepper had made it clear that I wasn't to call or come by Dolly's, so I stayed on the bench across the street and watched to make sure she was safe. I had typed out at least fifteen texts to her and deleted them in the past forty-eight hours. Sending her a fucking text didn't feel right.

She deserved more than that. I just needed my sister to leave the damn apartment so I could get close to her.

"I'll send Brick," I told her.

"What are you doing about Canyon?" she hissed.

"His ten days are almost up. We're going to find him," I replied, fighting the need to light up another cigarette. "He'll be handled soon."

Pepper let out a weary breath. "Take that crazy Mafia guy that everyone is so scared of with you."

She was mad at me, but she was still worried about me. That was a good sign.

"Presley," I replied. "He'll be there, along with some others."

"Okay, good. Then, you get that done. Don't get put in prison. And stay away from Dolly."

Only the first request I could promise, the second thing was a possibility, and the last one was a no. I was going to see Dolly, and Pepper was going to have to get the fuck over it.

"How is she?" I asked, staring at the window as if I could actually see shit this far away.

"Fine. Better. Why do you care?" She was annoyed. "Did you have a sudden stroke of guilt?"

"I care about her, Pep," I admitted.

It was possibly more than care. I was struggling with it. What I did know was that I missed her. I thought about her all the time. I wanted in that goddamn apartment so bad that I was close to snapping and going with Pepper in there so that I could see for myself that Dolly was okay.

Pepper was silent for a moment. I saw her walk out of the building and pinch her temples as she held the phone to her ear, not knowing I was watching her.

"Micah, she's fragile. You caring about her is not okay. She can't handle you and your ways."

"Why is she fragile, Pep?" I urged.

It had been keeping me up at night. Knowing there was shit in her head that was dark. Worrying that she was hurting herself and I wasn't there to stop it.

"Her past isn't an easy one. It's not something I talk about to anyone. Mom doesn't even know. Just…she has emotional trauma going back to when she was nine years old and her dad died."

Losing your dad was hard. I knew. But I couldn't say it had caused emotional trauma. She'd had a mom. One she seemed close to—or had been…I thought. I hadn't really paid much attention back then.

"Okay," I said, waiting for her to explain more.

I watched as my sister ran her hand over her head and stared up at the sky, as if she was struggling with what to say.

"We lost a dad too," I pushed, knowing she wanted to say more. I could see it in her body language.

"We didn't find ours hanging from a rope in the garage," she replied, and her shoulders slumped.

Fucking hell. The pain in my chest caused me to reach up and press against it with my hand.

Taking a deep breath, I looked back across the street at Pepper. "Her dad hung himself, and she found him…when she was nine?"

"Yes," she said with a deep sigh. "Yes, she did. But that is only the beginning. I can't tell you more. The rest is something she has trusted me with. The suicide you could find easily enough if you dug it up. It wasn't a secret."

How the fuck did it get worse than that? Why would a man do that in his home, where his child could find him?

"I need to see her, Pepper." I wasn't asking permission. I was just letting her know. At least when she found out I went over there the minute she left, she couldn't say I'd lied to her.

"She doesn't need to see you, Micah," she said sternly, and her entire body tensed.

I watched as she stalked toward her car, as if she were coming to find me and physically stop me.

"Why?" I asked.

"Because she's going through something, and I think it's because of you. I think it is you. That, or it's the combination of Canyon using her and you…you taking her virginity."

If she wanted me to stay away, that had been the wrong thing to say. No one was keeping me from her.

"If I'm the cause of it, then why can't I be the solution? Maybe she needs to see me. Ever think about that?"

Pepper slammed her car door shut. "Actually, I did. I considered it. But…this is you we are talking about. What Dolly needs, you can't give her."

"And what is that?" I shot back at her, waiting to see that Mustang disappear from sight so I could make my way over there.

"Unconditional love."

Well, fuck.

Twenty-Two

DOLLY

As my moka pot heated up, I stood in the kitchen, staring at the knife block. Pepper being here had been a distraction. She'd kept my mind occupied the best she could. But I was alone now. With my thoughts. The pain that had been there, slowly itching to grip hold of me, was no longer being pushed back.

Walking over to the knives, I took out the smallest one. The paring knife. I used it to peel apples. Staring down at it, I could already feel the relief it could bring me. I just had to slice a small piece of skin and let blood trickle out. Pepper wouldn't know. No one would.

I reached for the knob on the stove and turned off the gas eye. Espresso wasn't what I needed, and I knew it. Walking over to the closest kitchen chair, I sat down and pulled up my sundress. My gaze went to the marks I'd made with my nails.

They were almost gone, leaving nothing but faint marks of where they had been.

Pressing the tip of the knife on the upper part of my inner thigh, I moved it slowly, wincing as the sharp sting grew worse.

"One hundred twenty-two, one hundred twenty-two, one hundred twenty-two."

The thick blood oozed out, and I stopped as my eyes watered. I set the knife down on the table and let out a small sob as I watched the red trickle run down my leg. When it ran under my leg onto the seat, I covered my mouth in horror at what I'd let myself do. Again.

One hundred twenty-two, one hundred twenty-two, one hundred twenty-two.

It had been years since I'd done this. I had become a stronger person—or so I'd thought. The horror of my past I had shut away. Closed it off. Let it go. But now, here I was, opening the door. Shame, guilt, self-disgust all began to settle over me. It was as if old bullies had shown back up to taunt me. Some I knew all too well.

One hundred twenty-two, one hundred twenty-two, one hundred twenty-two.

Knocking at my door broke into my inner turmoil, and I stared in that direction, but I didn't get up. I wasn't in the right state of mind to deal with people. They'd go away. More knocking, then Micah's voice.

"Tink?"

Standing up, I started to go to him and paused, looking down as blood ran down to my knee. Turning, I rushed over to the sink to get a paper towel and wet it. I had to clean this up. I didn't want Micah to see me like this. I didn't want anyone to, but especially him. He'd know I was damaged.

He'd come to see me. That meant something. Right?

"Dolly!" he called louder and knocked again.

I had to hold the paper towel on the wound and apply pressure. I'd cut deeper than I'd intended. The sound of keys in the lock caused me to panic. The door opening and heavy footsteps had me moving faster. Taking the bloody paper towel, I turned and shoved it into the trash can.

"Dolly, where are you?" Micah sounded worried.

He would be horrified if he caught me like this. I had to clean up the blood on the floor, chair, and even table where the knife had been, but I didn't have time. Keeping him out of here was the only option. Grabbing another paper towel, I held it to the cut as I made my way out of the kitchen, then squeezed my thighs together to hold it there when I reached the living room.

Micah came walking back out of my bedroom at about that time. His eyes locked on me, and relief softened his tense expression. "Tink," he said with a sigh and made his way over to me. His eyes searching my face. "You've been crying."

Crap. I'd forgotten about that. I'd been more worried about the blood.

I shook my head and wiped at my face. "I'm fine," I assured him. "What're you doin' here?" I asked him.

He stopped in front of me. "I wanted to see you. I had to wait until Pep left."

"Why?"

He hadn't wanted to see me after we had sex.

He cupped my face in his hands and brushed his thumbs over my cheekbones. It was hard to remember why I shouldn't be letting him do this when he looked at me with those blue eyes like I was special.

"I missed you."

No. No, he was just saying that. I knew better. Pepper had been right all along. I was too naive. I shook my head.

"I'm not buying that, Micah Abe," I told him and tried to step back, but I felt the paper towel I'd forgotten between my legs and stopped before it fell to the ground.

"I need to explain," he said.

"No need. You can just go."

Hearing him tell me any excuse was dangerous. I was likely to fall for it hook, line, and sinker. Simply because I wanted it to be true.

"Tink, you don't mean that," he murmured as he ran a finger over my bottom lip. "You missed me too. Didn't you?"

Yes. I didn't tell him that though. I stayed silent.

"I want you to trust me," he whispered, staring down at my mouth.

He hadn't exactly done much to earn my trust. Or anything at all really. Except the fact that he'd been gentle during sex. He made it good for me. I had known it wasn't supposed to be good the first time—or even the first few times. I'd heard stories about it. Micah made sure it was special.

Then, he'd walked right out of the room, taking the bloodied sheets with him.

"You want me to trust you? I did. And then you left me alone to go tell...some blonde woman that I was boring and was bad at sex."

He narrowed his eyes. "What the fuck are you talking about? Blonde woman? Fucking Dylan? Did she come to my room?"

I just stared at him. He seemed sincere...sincerely pissed off.

I shook my head. "No. She stopped me on the stairs when I was leaving."

His nostrils flared, and his jaw clenched tightly.

"Tink, not one moment with you was boring. It was fucking spectacular. One time isn't gonna be close to enough for me."

"Did you come here to have sex again?" I blurted out.

He chuckled. "No. But once we've talked, if that's an option, then, yeah, baby, I'd like it very much."

My entire body began to tingle with anticipation. I had to stop this. I couldn't do this with him. Placing my hands on his chest, I shoved away from him. Before I could feel proud of myself, I felt panic instead. The paper towel fell to the floor, and I froze. There was a chance he wouldn't notice. I could steer him toward the door. Tell him I wanted to be alone. That I needed time to get over it.

His eyes narrowed, as if he was trying to read my thoughts. He tilted his head as he looked at me. A strand of his blond hair that wasn't long enough to fit in the ponytail fell over the side of his face. Then, his gaze trailed down my body until it stopped on the floor.

For a moment, it was like watching this all play out in slow motion. I had to say or do something.

When he bent to pick up the bloody paper towel, I took another step away from him. Lies began forming in my head, and I tried to think of the most believable one. I started to open my mouth to spout it out when he grabbed my leg with one hand and jerked my sundress up with another.

I attempted to squeeze my legs together, but he pulled it open, then sucked in a sharp breath.

"Tink," he said tightly, "what did you do?"

I struggled to grab on to an excuse and verbalize it. They all seemed weak and unbelievable. I shook my head instead of saying anything. Micah stood up, his entire body now rigid as he grabbed my hand and began walking me toward the kitchen.

No, no, no, no, no. This was bad.

I pulled back on my arm, trying to slow him or redirect him.

His hand wrapped around my wrist and continued to tug me with him. When he walked into the room, he froze.

His hand squeezed my wrist and then let go. "What the fuck, Dolly?" he whispered.

I closed my eyes and turned to run out of the room, but he was quicker than I was. His hands grabbed my waist and stopped me. The ragged breath he took as he held me quietly for a moment told me he was struggling with this. The lump in my throat was there instantly.

One hundred twenty-two, one hundred twenty-two, one hundred twenty-two, one hundred twenty-two, one hundred twenty-two, one hundred twenty-two.

"Why, Tink?" His voice was thick with emotion.

I closed my eyes and swallowed hard. "I don't know," I lied. I knew. I'd had hundreds of hours of counseling that taught me why and how to overcome it.

He pressed his face into my hair. "Please, tell me how to fix it." He sounded as if he was in pain.

I shook my head. "You can't."

We stood there silently, and he turned me around to face him before pulling me into his chest and holding me. I could hear his heart pounding rapidly. My hands fisted in his shirt, and I clung to him as the tears came and the lump began to ease.

He reached down and scooped me up, then walked back to the living room, carrying me over to the sofa, where he sat down and continued to cradle me in his arms. He rested his forehead on the top of my head. "I will maim, kill, torture, whatever I need to do to whoever caused this if you will just tell me why, who. Point me in the right direction. Something. Just give me something here, Tink."

I stared at his arm wrapped around me. There was no one he could do any of those things to in order to fix this. Even if my aunt were still alive, him harming her the way…she had done to me…it wouldn't heal what she had damaged. That was permanent. The past couldn't be rewritten.

"There is no one," I said, turning my head so that he could see the truth in my eyes. "Nothing you can do will erase history."

He was silent a moment before saying, "Tell me. If I know, I can help you. I will help you. I never want you to hurt your body again. I can't stand it, Tink. This perfect skin is… precious."

I had two options here. Tell him the truth, which meant trusting another person with my secrets. Or refuse to open up and possibly push away a guy I didn't want to leave.

Twenty-Three

MICAH

I wanted to rage. Destroy something. Tear the wall down brick by brick. The only thing holding me together was Dolly in my arms.

Pepper had said she was fragile. She knew about this. She had stayed, for fear of Dolly doing this to herself.

My arms tightened around her, and I watched as her shoulders rose and fell with a deep breath.

"When I was nine years old…" she began, and I realized what she was about to tell me.

Part of me wanted to tuck her in my arms and carry her far away from that memory. Tell her not to say it. I didn't want to cause her any more pain. But the sane part of me knew she was trusting me. She was opening up, and I had to let her do this. I needed to know. If I was going to help her, I had to know what I was dealing with.

I reached for her hand and threaded my fingers through hers, then held it firmly. With her eyes locked on our hands, she seemed to relax some.

"It was my dad's forty-ninth birthday. My mom was making his favorite meal—meatloaf. She'd made him a buttercream cake the night before, and I was so excited about getting to eat a piece after church. I'd made him a card." She paused as a sad smile came and went just as quickly to her lips. "I went to find him and give it to him. He…he had gone out to the garage earlier, and he did that often to tinker with his model cars and listen to the radio. He liked country music, and Momma believed it was a sin, so he only played it out at his work-bench with the volume real low. He was good about things like that. Respecting Momma's beliefs when I don't think he really agreed with her much. He never said it though."

She took a deep breath and let it out slowly. I prepared myself for the rest. I knew it was coming, but I wasn't sure I could handle seeing the pain on her face as she told me. My thumb caressed hers as I waited.

"He had taken the green rope, which he used every Decem-ber to tie the Christmas tree to the roof of our Volvo wagon, to hang himself. I…I found him there. In the garage. Hang-ing by that rope. I think I was in shock. I remember feeling sick, then numb. I had to tell Momma. Someone had to get him down. It looked awful. It was a terrible sight to see.

"I went back to the kitchen to tell Momma, and the dread of her reaction when she saw him made every step I took harder and harder. I counted them. Those steps. Every last step I counted. From the spot where I had found him until I stopped in the kitchen to tell my momma that Daddy was hanging in the garage. One hundred twenty-two." She whis-pered the number. "One hundred twenty-two steps.

"Momma raced to him, screaming and wailing. The rest gets blurry. Our neighbor heard her, and he came. The cops came. Church people came and brought food.

"The next few weeks, Momma closed herself away. She didn't eat much. When I tried to get her to, she refused. She rarely left her room. When I hadn't shown up for school in two weeks, they finally called, but I answered. They wanted to talk to Momma, but she wouldn't pick up the phone.

"That was when...that was when my dad's older sister, Naola, came to stay with us. She was stern and even more religious than Momma."

Dolly stopped talking again and shifted in my lap. The faraway look in her expression as she continued to stare at our hands was breaking my heart.

"Aunt Naola had never come around much when my daddy was alive. I found out soon enough it was because she didn't approve of my momma...and, by extension, me. While Momma stayed locked in her room, Aunt Naola decided to right the evil in me—or that is what she called it. She...she told me my daddy had hung himself because he saw no other way out of the life he had. That he was stuck with me and Momma and he preferred eternal hell over us."

"She would tell me my momma was crazy, mental, and that I had her disease. We had a devil in us, and he'd eventually kill us, the way we had killed my daddy." She inhaled deeply and let it out. "She would get me out of bed at night and tell me the demons had come for me. Then, she'd push me out onto the back porch and lock the door. Leaving me there with the demons. They never came, of course, but I was terrified nonetheless."

She shook her head and pressed her lips together before turning to look at me. "That's all I can talk about right now," she whispered. "I don't want to talk about the rest."

Fuck. I wasn't sure I could take much more of it. I pulled her against my chest, and she let go of my hand and wrapped her arms around my neck.

"A month after Aunt Naola came to stay with us, I started cutting myself with my daddy's pocketknife I had found in his workbench."

I kissed her head and didn't press for more. She'd told me more than my sister, and I knew letting me into her dark past had been hard.

"People commit suicide because of mental instability, things they struggle with, a sickness they lose control over. Your dad didn't kill himself because of you," I told her, needing her to believe me.

She nodded. "I know."

So then, that hadn't made her want to harm her body today. "Why did you cut yourself today, Tink?" I asked, brushing her hair back so I could see her face.

"To get the pain out," she replied.

"What pain?"

She closed her eyes. "Of never being enough."

Fucking hell.

Twenty-Four

DOLLY

I opened my eyes and looked around my bedroom. It was then I heard the voices. Sitting up, I winced at the sting between my thighs, then looked down to see the bandage Micah had put there after he doctored it. He had made me swear to never do it again. That I was to call him if I ever had the urge to do it and he'd come running. After that, he laid me on the bed and curled up behind me. The emotional morning had exhausted me, and I'd fallen asleep.

"You promised you would leave her alone!" Pepper's voice carried through the closed door.

"No, I didn't. Think back on that conversation. I had no intentions of leaving her alone. When you called, I was sitting on the fucking bench across the street, waiting on you to leave," Micah replied.

I stood up and moved closer to the door, not sure if I needed to go out there and stop this or not.

"What part of *she's fragile* do you not get? Stop being so… so selfish!"

"Don't." Micah's voice lowered. "You're about to cross a line, sis. You need to step back. Dolly is dealing with shit. She's been through a lot. I get it. I'm not here to fuck her. I'm here to take care of her. To help her. To make sure she doesn't cut herself again."

"Since when do you take care of women?" Pepper snapped.

"I'm not the bastard you seem to think I am."

"Micah, I don't think you're a bastard. I just know you can't be what she needs."

"Yeah, the fuck I can."

"Is that so?" she replied. "You realize that Dolly needs—"

I swung open the door to stop whatever was about to come out of Pepper's mouth. Their heads turned at the same time, and both sets of eyes locked on me.

I forced a smile. "Y'all mind if I decide what it is I do and do not need?"

Pepper looked remorseful, but Micah continued to study me.

"I'm sorry, Dolly," Pepper said.

Micah walked over to me. His eyes never leaving my face. "And what is it that you need, Tink?" he asked.

That list could be interesting. I saw the teasing gleam in his eye, and I smiled.

"Right now, I need a cheeseburger with extra pickles and fries. Maybe some caramel doughnuts."

He chuckled. "I can manage that."

"Great. You two just laugh and act like this isn't a disaster waiting to happen. One I will have to clean up," Pepper said, crossing her arms over her chest as she glared at Micah, then looked at me with concern.

"I am failing to see how my being here to help her and be her friend is a potential for disaster," Micah told her.

"Oh, let's see. Two days ago, you took her virginity. That's a friendship sure to blossom." Sarcasm dripped from her words.

My face warmed, and I looked down at the floor. I hadn't expected her to go there.

"Tink?" Micah slid a finger under my chin and lifted my face up to meet his. "Did you like sex? Did I make you feel good?"

Now, my face was on fire. My eyes widened, and he grinned at me.

"Come on. Tell her the truth."

"Micah!" Pepper scolded.

"I enjoyed it," I replied just above a whisper.

"And today, did I try to do anything more than comfort you?"

I shook my head.

He looked back at Pepper. "See? I'm here to be whatever she needs. I left her with you for two days, and the moment you left, she was slicing up that pretty skin of hers. Not happening again. I won't let it. You failed at helping her. I won't."

"Shut up!" Pepper shouted, then pointed to the door. "Go. Just leave. I got this."

Micah didn't budge. He shook his head. "No."

"Micah, so help me GOD!"

Stepping between them, I held up my hands. "Both of you, stop," I pleaded. "Right now, I should send you both away, but I can't promise I won't get weak and pathetic. I might cut myself because I'm not okay. I hate it. I hate it so much. The truth is, I want someone here until I know I have this under control. Should it be Micah?" I paused and looked at him. "Probably not." Then, I looked at Pepper. "But you can't be here all the time either. I have two jobs. I will try to get more shifts. Or a third job. I don't know. I do know I hate feeling like I'm a burden, but I'm willing to admit I need help. And"—I dropped my shoulders and sighed—"I really don't wanna go back to my momma's."

Micah stepped toward me, and I held my hand up to stop him.

"I will be here when you are home. I will be wherever you need me to be. You just call me."

God, I needed him to stop being so sweet. It was making this harder.

"I am her best friend. I will be here. You go handle that cocksucker that started all this."

A knock at the door caused all our heads to turn in that direction. Walking past them both, I headed to open it.

"Wait, Tink. I'll get it," Micah said, stepping around me to grab the knob.

"I can open my own door," I informed him.

He winked at me. "Easy, tiger."

I was scowling at his back when he opened my door. The large bouquet of bright pink, blue, yellow, and orange flowers almost completely hid the delivery boy's head.

"These are for Dolly Dixon," he said, holding them out.

Micah was glaring at him as if the boy himself had sent me flowers.

I moved around Micah and reached for them. "Thank you."

"You're welcome," he replied nervously before hurrying to get away from Micah.

"Who are they from?" Pepper demanded.

I walked over and set them on the table beside the door. Micah reached for the small envelope before I could and started opening it.

When he jerked the card out, he read it, and his jaw clenched tightly. "Motherfucker."

"Canyon," Pepper said matter-of-factly.

Micah barely nodded as he wadded the card up into his fist. "I'll take them to the dumpster," he said, reaching for them.

I liked flowers, and it felt like a waste. They'd been cut, and they should at least be enjoyed. But Canyon had hurt Pepper, and I agreed they had to go.

"Wait. Can I give them to Mrs. Mildred? She'd enjoy them."

Micah stared at me as if he wanted to argue.

"If the flowers are gonna die, I just hate for their life to have been cut in vain. Let them brighten up someone's life while they still can," I explained.

He nodded and then smirked.

"I'll take them to her," Pepper offered. "Dolly is right."

Relieved, I was glad that I didn't have to fight about that.

"Back to the current situation," Pepper said. "I need to get back to the bar. Micah, you need to go find Canyon and deal with him. Make him a nonissue."

"I will. But not right now. I'm not leaving Tink alone."

Pepper looked at me, then finally seemed to give in. "Fine. Stay with her. I'll come back tonight."

I was starting to feel like a child being tossed back and forth between bickering parents.

"You said you couldn't stay tonight when we talked on the phone earlier," Micah said pointedly.

She shot him a look I couldn't see, and he smirked.

"That was when I thought you'd send someone other than yourself to stay with her." Pepper walked over to me and hugged me. "Be careful," she whispered and kissed my cheek.

I knew she meant, *Don't get emotionally attached to my brother.*

I nodded.

She glared at Micah. "Be good."

He saluted her, then went and opened the door for her. "Bye."

Pepper paused and gave him one last warning look before taking the flowers and leaving.

When he closed the door, he turned back to me. "Go brush your hair so it doesn't look like I just fucked you, and let's go get some burgers."

I reached up and felt my hair. It was messy from my nap. "Okay," I agreed.

Getting out of this apartment was probably a good thing.

Twenty-Five

MICAH

"I wish you'd let me drive," I said, not liking the idea of Dolly walking so much with her thigh sliced the way it was.

"It was just around the corner, and you only have your bike here, and my battery is dead from not being driven. I probably need a new one anyway."

"Tink, it wasn't just around the corner. It's almost a mile there and back. Besides, was your experience on the back of Tex's ride that bad that you don't want to try it again?"

She flashed those almond-shaped amber eyes at me, then turned her attention straight ahead again. "Last I heard, you don't let bitches on the back of your bike. I was unaware it was an option."

I slapped her ass with a firm pop, causing her to jump and squeal, then level me with a glare.

"I'd had a bad day, Tink. Don't go throwing stupid shit in my face that I might have said when my temper was up. You're not a bitch, and you're an exception to my rule."

The way the corners of her mouth twitched, I could tell she wanted to smile.

"You never told me I'd graduated from bitch to exception." She paused then and pointed across the street. "We gotta go back that way."

It added at least eight hundred more feet. I was worried the bandage she had on wasn't enough, and I didn't want her leg bleeding anymore.

"Give me a good reason before I toss you over my shoulder and take you back the shorter way."

She pointed, then waved with a bright smile on her face before looking back at me and holding up the bag with an extra burger and fries she had ordered. "That's where Harold is tonight. I gotta take him his supper."

When she had asked for one to go, I'd assumed she was going to take it home for tomorrow. I should have figured out this was her feeding the homeless again. Nodding, I waved a hand for her to lead the way, and I fell into step just far enough behind her to have a good view of her ass.

Being with Dolly was unique experience for me. For starters, I fucking enjoyed it. She made things seem…brighter. Watching the animated way she talked when she told me a story and listening to her laugh when I cracked a joke…I was starting to need it. I'd thought I only liked women for one thing. Once that need was met, I didn't require them. But with Dolly, it was more than what her tight little cunt did for me. I just simply wanted to be near her. It was intriguing as hell.

When I'd been seventeen, I had been in love. The only time. But I always figured it was because I'd been young and stupid. That I hadn't known the drama attached to a woman yet. Calista and I had been friends for years before it became more. I mean, I was a guy, and she was gorgeous. Our friendship became an issue. At least for me. I wanted her. Maybe it was more teenage lust than anything, but the connection we'd had growing up made it more. When she had left, I'd been fucking pathetic.

Dolly wasn't the first female since Calista that I enjoyed being around. There had been Fawn. She'd been older than me and drama free. At least until she caught me cheating on her and left me. Now, she was married to the fucking Mafia boss. Or former boss. His son was the official boss now.

"What do you have for me there?" the older man asked, standing up from the crate he had been sitting on with a rolled-up newspaper in his hand, smiling at Dolly.

"Cheeseburger and fries. Still nice and warm," she informed him, handing him the bag. "I'm sorry I haven't been out to check on you. Did your things survive the storm?"

The man opened the paper bag and inhaled deeply. "Sure did. I ain't got much, and what I did have, I stored away 'fore I went on to the shelter. They fed me up right. Didn't go without. I rationed it up like I do and made it work up till I finished the rest of this mornin'. You came just in time."

I could see the relief shining in Dolly's eyes as he spoke.

"Harold, this is my friend Micah," Dolly began, and my eyes met Harold's.

"I know 'im already. He's the one that took me to the shelter. Nice one it was. I ain't ever stayed somewhere that took such good care of folks like us." He nodded his head at me. "Thank ye for that."

"You're welcome," I replied, feeling Dolly's eyes now locked on me.

"Well, uh…I'm, uh, glad they were so good to you," Dolly said slowly. I could tell her mind was working a mile a minute with the way she was struggling with what to say. "Enjoy that burger then. All of it. I'll have something for you out here tomorrow."

"I'll do it, Miss Dolly," he replied.

I finally met Dolly's expressive eyes, and I could see the gratitude in them. I hadn't done it for her to be grateful to me. I did it because she cared about the man. I hadn't really thought about why I was helping him when I gone to find him. Looking at her face now, I was really fucking glad I had.

"Ready?" I asked.

She nodded her head, then looked back at Harold and said her goodbyes before we headed toward the apartment.

"I don't know what to say," she said softly.

"You could thank me," I teased lightly.

"Thank you. I mean, of course I am thankful. I just feel like that isn't enough."

"It is, Tink," I assured her.

Twenty-Six

DOLLY

Strong arms cradled me and lifted me up from the sofa, where I'd fallen asleep, watching a movie with Micah. The living room was dark, but I could still see Micah's jawline and muscular neck with the moonlight shining through the windows.

"I was trying not to wake you," he said as he walked me back to the bedroom.

"I'm sorry I fell asleep," I replied.

"Don't be. You're cute when you sleep. I enjoyed it."

There was the *cute* word again, except this time, I wasn't as annoyed with it. Not when he was carrying me to my bed. He set me down on and looked around the room, and then his eyes swung back to me.

"Where can I find your pajamas?" he asked.

I was still in my sundress from today. Was he going to get the pajamas and step out of the room or watch me change?

Did it matter? He'd seen me naked already. Yes, it mattered. That had been different. He would be really seeing me, not distracted with sex this time.

"I can get them," I said, starting to get up.

Placing his hands on my shoulders, he stopped me. "No, Tink. I'll get them. Where are they?"

Tonight had been…perfect. We didn't argue once. He made me laugh and was attentive. I'd never felt like I was annoying him or that he wanted to be somewhere else. The thought of messing that up by refusing to let him help me get changed for bed kept me from arguing.

"Top drawer of the dresser, on the left," I replied, giving in as my stomach began to flutter with nerves.

He turned and walked over to open it.

"The pink one on top will be fine," I told him when he didn't move to take a nightgown out.

"You sleep in this?" he asked, reaching in to take out the first satin gown, then held it up with both hands to inspect it.

My face heated, and I felt more exposed than I had thought I would. I liked pretty nighties. I always had. It made me happy. Even if there was no one to see them on me.

When I didn't respond, Micah turned around to me with the satin gown in his hand. "The only thing that should surprise me is that they aren't all pink," he said, walking back over to me. "After seeing that insanely feminine robe you had on the morning I woke up here and the panties and bra I took off you the other night, I should have known my Tink wears dainty, little, feminine nighties to bed."

My Tink.

I felt my heart do a crazy jolt at those words.

When he reached me, he nodded his head. "Stand up."

As if I was completely under his command, I did as told.

Micah laid the nightgown on the bed beside me, then took the hem of my sundress and lifted it up and off my body. I stopped breathing when he dropped it to the floor. His gaze traveled down my bare chest to the ice-blue lace panties I was wearing. The way his neck flexed as he swallowed before trailing his gaze back up my body made my nipples pebble, and I shivered.

"Get in bed, Tink," he said in a raspy voice.

Wanting to cover up, I reached for the nightgown, and he snatched it from my hands.

"You won't be needing that."

This meant…we were going to have sex again. At least, that was what I hoped it meant. I scooted back on the bed until I was in the center of my queen-size mattress. Micah began to remove his clothes with such swift movements that I wanted to ask him to slow down so I could enjoy the show. If I were more secure or self-assured, I would have done just that.

"I didn't stay to fuck you. I stayed to take care of you. I wanted to hold you while you slept and know you were okay. Should've known once I got in this bedroom with you, all my goodwill would go to hell. As if you're not tempting enough, you have a drawer of sexy little nighties that no man has seen on you." Micah climbed on the bed and knelt over me. His appreciative gaze made me feel special.

When his fingers brushed the new bandage he'd put on my thigh after we walked back to the apartment, I saw him wince, as if the sight pained him.

"Promise me, Tink, fucking swear to me, that I'll never have to see you hurt your body again," he whispered as his eyes lifted back to meet mine.

I wanted to promise him anything, but I also didn't want to lie. What if I couldn't? What if I had opened up this addictive need and it was going to take years of therapy for me to control it again?

Micah's fingers slid into the sides of my panties, and he tugged them down my hips, then thighs, being extra careful of my wound before pulling them the rest of the way off.

"Jesus Christ, you're beautiful," he murmured, then moved over my body, lowering himself until his mouth covered mine.

He tasted of mint and whiskey. Reaching up, I grabbed his arms and felt his muscles flex beneath my touch. He licked at my bottom lip and groaned before sinking back into the kiss, giving me more of his talented tongue.

His hand ran down the side of my hip, then over my stomach before he slipped his fingers between my legs. Opening me and caressing the ache that he had caused to stir. My hips lifted of their own accord. I wanted more, knowing what else he could do to me. Craving it like I did my next breath.

"So wet," he said as he kissed the corner of my mouth. "So sweet," he murmured, trailing his gentle pecks down my neck and collarbone until he reached my breasts. He began to suck on one of my nipples as his fingers squeezed and caressed the other one.

He was everywhere, it seemed, and my body was humming with pleasure. I was sure in this moment that he could ask me anything, and I'd agree to it. Just to have him here. Keep him with me in this bed. Nothing had ever made me feel the way he did.

When he began to pump his fingers in and out of me, I felt the world fall away and center on him at the same time. I wanted more. My body was desperate for the feel of him inside me. Filling me, stretching me to the bite of pain that would soon be taken over by bliss.

"I don't want to hurt you, baby," he groaned, as he watched me moving against his hand, trying to take more.

"Please, Micah," I pleaded. "I need…"

"Tell me, Tink. What do you need?" he urged.

I gasped for air, and my eyes found his. "You. Please. Inside me."

He hissed, then shoved my unharmed thigh up and to the side, opening me wider. He ran his knuckles along my opening and caused me to cry out as he circled the most sensitive spot between my legs with his thumb.

"Micah!" I cried, grabbing at the sheets and lifting my hips again.

He moved then, his arms flexing as they held him over my body. His perfect teeth bit down on his lower lip as he thrust inside of me. The invasion was what I'd wanted, but there was still a sharp pain that came with it. Throwing my head back, I cried out, but didn't pull away. I wanted him there. I never wanted him to leave.

"GODDAMN, Tink!" he shouted, then began to move. Sinking deeper, then withdrawing and doing it again.

I was lost in the sensation. The promise of paradise and the sheer beauty of the man inside of me. The veins on his neck stood out as his entire body flexed with each glorious movement. If this was a sin, I was one hundred percent sure it was worth going to hell over.

"Nothing," he growled. "Nothing has ever felt this fucking incredible."

His eyes stared down at me. The black of his pupils almost dominating all of the blue of his irises. Seeing his pleasure triggered something, and the euphoria exploded inside of me.

My vision blurred, and I clung to his arms as the powerful tremors overtook me. I heard him say my name, but I was lost to this. Everything about it.

"FUUUCK!" he let out in a roar before jerking back and pulling out of me.

I wanted to reach for him and pull him back, but the warm sensation that hit my stomach snapped me from my crazed rapture. My eyes flew open, and I watched as Micah pumped his release onto me. His chest heaved with each shot that came out of him.

"Goddammit," he swore when he finally stopped and stilled, panting as he stared down at the semen on my skin. His eyes closed for a moment, and he inhaled a deep, ragged breath. "Shit. I didn't mean to."

He lifted his eyes to mine, and I saw the whirl of emotions there.

"I never forget. I don't fuck without a condom. I swear. I get tested regularly. But I'll take us both to get checked. I got—" He ran a hand through his hair and let out a weary sigh. "Dammit, Tink. I'm sorry. I shouldn't have gotten so carried away. I should have thought."

I listened to him, understanding that he was worried about not having used a condom, but he'd pulled out. The cum was on me, not in me. The only thing bothering me was…he seemed to think we needed to get checked.

"I'll clean you up," he said, climbing off the bed and walking, naked, toward my bathroom.

I lay there, not sure if I should have said something or if I was missing something. He seemed more concerned than I would have liked.

Had he…had he had sex since we had a few days ago? When was the last time he had gotten checked? And was I jealous—because he'd had sex recently enough with someone else—more than I was worried about getting an STD?

When he returned, he paused and looked down at me. The damp cloth was fisted in his hand. "I should be feeling like a bastard right now, but seeing my cum on your pretty skin only makes me want to rub it all over you," he said hoarsely. Then, he looked up to meet my gaze. "I want to see my cum leaking out of your cunt, Tink. I came real damn close to unloading that inside you."

I let out a shaky breath. If he had, this would have been a much different conversation. As much as I loved seeing the territorial gleam in his eye, there was one problem with that scenario. I had never taken birth control a day in my life. I hadn't needed it. I'd figured when the time came for sex, we would use a condom.

Now understanding how different it felt with him bare, I got the need for birth control. I wanted to do that again. I wanted him to come inside me. I wanted to see him look at me like that while we were still joined.

He began to clean my stomach, then between my legs before tossing the cloth to the floor.

"Sit up," he instructed me. "Let me pull the covers back."

I did so, helping him get them out from under my butt, then slid beneath them as he climbed in beside me. I was unsure what it was he needed me to say. I wasn't sorry we'd had sex, and honestly, the sight of him shooting his cum onto me wasn't one I wanted to ever forget.

Micah slid his knuckle under my chin and tilted my head back to look at him. "You're not on any birth control, are you?"

I hesitated, then shook my head.

"I was just tested two weeks ago. I've been with someone else since then, other than you. I used a condom though.

I always use a condom. You're safe. I promise, but I'll get checked just to give you some reassurance."

Again, I should be concerned about the STD thing, but I wasn't. Not when he had just admitted to sleeping with some other woman. I was more focused on the when. Had it been before us or in between our two times? I felt a sick knot in my stomach and wished I didn't care.

"Say something, Tink," he urged.

I blinked up at him. What did I say? I'd just had the best sexual experience of my life—not that I had many to compare it to, but I seriously doubted it got better than that—and he wanted to discuss his sex life with other girls and getting tested for sexually transmitted diseases.

He brushed his thumb over my bottom lip. "I can see your brain spinning. Your eyes give you away. Just talk to me."

Okay. Fine. Just be blunt. He sure is.

"Have you had sex with another woman since we slept together?" I asked.

The right corner of his mouth twitched slightly. If I hadn't been studying him so closely, I would have missed it.

"That's what has that unhappy frown puckering your brows?" he asked with an amused tone.

I started to turn away from him, angry that he was going to tease me about this. He'd asked, and I had been honest. Now, he was going to make light of it.

His arm clamped down over my waist, holding me in my place. "Oh, no, you don't. Stop getting all worked up into a snit."

I glared at him. "You asked me, and then you made me feel like an idiot when I told you the truth."

He leaned down and rested his forehead against mine. "That wasn't what I meant to do. I'm sorry. I just hadn't expected that to be what you were worried about. The answer is no. I've not touched a woman or looked in her fucking direction since you were in my bed. I swear."

"Oh," I whispered.

He kissed the corner of my mouth. "We need to get you on birth control," he said softly, then pressed a kiss to my chin. "Because now that I've had you raw, I'm gonna need it every time."

I shivered as his hand slid over my stomach where his cum had been.

"Every time?" I asked.

"Mmhmm," was his reply as he began to trace circles over my skin. "As much as I liked seeing my cum on you, I want it *in* you more. The thought of knowing you're walking around with damp panties from my cum makes me feel some strong shit I'm not ready to put a name to just yet."

Oh good Lord. How was I going to survive this man?

Twenty-Seven

MICAH

The Hendricks was known for two things: the place to get any fix you needed and prostitution. It paraded as a strip club, but had been raided and shut down several times over the years. New "ownership" would take over, and it always seemed to go undetected for a while until the DA got wind of it, and then it happened all over again.

"You sure this is where Canyon is hiding out?" I asked Levi Shephard as we stepped down into the underground entrance to the club behind Gage Presley and another one of the family members, Huck Kingston.

Liam had called and said Blaise was ready for this to be finished and was sending his top three men. Once we were inside, The Judgment members that we'd brought along would surround the parking lot. However, I was the only one going inside with the Mafia. That had been Liam's call.

"I put a tracker on him three days ago. I'm positive," he replied.

Of course he had. These men were on another playing level when it came to shit like this. Where we would barge in with our guns and demand shit, they would have things already set in place to ensure it went their way. It was smart, but rarely did we deal with this kind of thing. They were experts at getting what was owed to them.

"Blaise know the sick fucker in charge has underage girls here he's pimping out?" Gage asked.

"Yes, I gave him all the info I could pull off their private servers," Levi replied.

"Then, if I slice his neck open, he'll understand," Gage said.

The massive man built like a damn brick wall, Huck Kingston, turned his head to look back at Gage. "You're not slicing anyone today. We came to get the fucking money. If Boss wants us to stop the underage shit, then we set that up and come handle it."

"If my blade slips," Gage drawled.

Huck shot him a warning look before turning back to the door.

"Nine, five, three, F-R-S, seven, pound," Levi told Huck.

He pressed the code into the keypad at the door. I didn't question how the fuck they knew it. They seemed to know everything.

The door clicked, and Huck pushed it open.

We all filed in with Levi being the last one inside. We had come in through some back entrance, seeing as there would have been no way they'd let us in the main door without bloodshed. The room we were in looked like a cellar.

"Through there," Levi instructed. "Huck, you go first. I don't trust Gage not to kill some fucker."

Huck moved in front of Gage, who smirked as if he found it amusing. I wasn't sure anyone could keep that psycho from killing if he wanted to, but I didn't know them all that well. Maybe they knew how to handle him.

The beat of the music was faint, but the farther we walked down the dark hallway, the closer it seemed. I knew that the plan was that we were all going to go in as undetected as possible, find Canyon and surround him.

Motherfucking pink roses had been outside Tink's door this morning. I'd found them and dropped them off outside Mrs. Mildred's door on my way to get Tink's caramel doughnuts before taking her to work.

Admitting that I was more pissed about him still going after Dolly, like he had a chance, than the fucker owing the club a hundred grand was something I tried not to focus on. The past three days and nights with Dolly had been perfect. I couldn't remember a time I had ever been this fucking happy.

Pepper wasn't speaking to me after I had the lock changed on Tink's apartment and refused to let her inside. But she'd get over it. We'd get it worked out soon. I had just wanted some time with Tink before I dealt with my sister. Explaining to her this was different for me was going to be difficult, considering I didn't have a real understanding of it yet either.

I just knew I missed Tink when she wasn't with me. I thought about her all damn day, and I wasn't even freaking out about it.

"Up those stairs, to the left," Levi instructed behind me.

"How do you know your way around this place?" I asked, amazed.

"He's lethal when it comes to finding out shit. Give him an hour, and he will have every secret you've ever had printed out and in a file," Gage said, then chuckled.

The music was louder now, pumping heavy behind the door. Huck opened it and moved slowly into the main area of the club while we filed in behind him. He glanced back at Gage and nodded once. Gage grinned and walked toward the bar as if he owned the place. No fear. His hand wasn't even on the gun tucked away at his side.

"There," Levi said, pointing to the booths to the right of the bar. "He's alone."

Huck walked off in the opposite direction, and Levi looked at me.

"Let's go get the money," he said, then started toward Canyon.

I'd never been in this place, but from the money I knew these fuckers made with their illegal shit, they could afford to keep the place clean. It looked like it hadn't been updated in twenty years. I fell into step beside Levi, who was acting as if we'd come to get a beer and watch the stripper onstage.

The closer we got to Canyon, who was leaning back in his booth, staring down at his phone, the more agitated I got. He'd kissed and touched Tink. She'd liked him. Had she thought she was in love with him? The thought made my stomach turn. I hated the sight of the fucker, but the idea of him having any hold on Tink caused rage to build with each step closer to him I took.

We were almost to him when his head snapped up, and his eyes locked on us. He reached for his gun, and I watched his entire body tense up.

Levi shook his head at him. "I wouldn't do that," he warned.

Canyon's eyes shot from me and back to Levi, and then they scanned the room. I could tell the moment he spotted Gage. There was a slight pale color that came over his complexion. I enjoyed it immensely.

Levi slid in the booth across from him, and I sat down beside him.

"I got shit to do, Acree," Levi told him. "And seeing as one warning wasn't enough for you, the boss has sent us out to make sure this is the last time. Now, you can take your hand off the gun and put both your hands up on the table so we can see them, or Gage can take you out from his spot at the bar."

Canyon stared at Levi before slowly moving his hands back onto the table. "I don't have the money yet."

"Bullshit," Levi replied with a grin that was more evil than amused. "The Crowns have the money. Now, you can pay the Judgment back, or I can hand you over to Gage. He brought his knife, and he's a little more than pissed off about the underage girls being used here. I'd steer clear of him if I were you."

Canyon shook his head. "I don't have shit to do with what they do here."

"Didn't say you did. Won't matter to Gage either. He just likes to slice folks up. He's a sick fucker like that."

Canyon looked at me. "It's not that easy. I can't just take a hundred grand from the club," he said. "You know shit doesn't work that way."

"Then, it sounds like they'll be needing a new VP soon," I replied. "At least then, the fucking flowers will stop."

His eyes narrowed slightly as he looked at me.

"When I left Dolly's apartment this morning, I made sure to drop them off at the neighbor's," I said, grinning. Relishing the fact that he knew I'd been there with her. She wasn't his. She was never gonna be his.

"This ain't about Dolly. Leave her out of this," he said as his hands fisted on the table.

"I won't be leaving her or her bed anytime soon," I informed him.

Canyon's face turned red, and he started to stand up, but Levi cleared his throat.

"Sudden moves aren't smart," he warned him.

Canyon's eyes shot back over to Gage, and he swallowed hard, lowering himself back into the booth.

"As entertaining as this drama unfolding is, I have better things to do. Where is the money, Acree? You were told ten days, and you got eleven."

"I said, I don't have it," he snarled at Levi.

"That's not good," he replied, then nodded at me to get up.

I stood, and Levi moved out of the seat. Canyon was watching us carefully as one of his hands slid back under the table. I started to say something, but Levi looked back at him.

"I'll tell him to start with your dick," he informed Canyon, then began walking away.

I stood there, unsure what the fuck was going on, when Gage began walking over in our direction.

"I can get it. Just let me go handle some things." The fear in Canyon's voice made it tremble as he moved to get up.

"Too late," Gage replied with a villainous curl to his lips.

"Wait. I'm sorry. He threw me off, talking about fucking Dolly. I'll go get it."

Gage didn't look at me, but kept his eyes on Canyon. "Well then, you can think about how he's fucking her while I show you how pretty my blade is."

"Let's go," Levi called after me.

I turned back to see him waiting on me near the main entrance.

Heading in his direction, I heard Canyon whimper. Was he slicing him up in here? In front of witnesses? I decided not to look back.

"What happens next?" I asked Levi as we walked outside past the bouncers, who seemed to give Levi a wide berth, as if they knew exactly who he was.

"Gage and Huck will take him out the back. Make sure he hands over the money and stays the fuck away from your sister's best friend…which is what I was told she was." His gaze looked amused as he said the last part. "Will we be needing to save you from your sister, too, Abe, or can you handle that on your own?"

I let out a sigh, then laughed. "I'll let you know."

Twenty-Eight

DOLLY

"Uh, smoking-hot biker guy, whose abs I would pay to lick, is asking for you," Zander said, sticking his head in the door to the book return room.

I set down the current book I was checking back in and grinned.

"He's early," I told him. "Could you send him back here to me? I have five more books, and then I'll be done."

Zander raised his eyebrows at me. "He's picking you up? As in you are leaving with a sexy biker man?"

I nodded, pressing my lips together to keep from laughing. "Yes, he is."

"Damn, girl, look at Little Miss Prim and Proper being naughty," he replied before closing the door and leaving me to finish my work.

It was hard to focus though, knowing Micah was here. This morning, he had brought me my favorite caramel doughnuts to bed, then taken one of them and rubbed the caramel off it and onto several places on my body before licking it off.

The harder I tried to protect my heart from getting hurt, the more difficult he made it. I wanted to be with him all the time. When he smiled at me, the world seemed to glow. My heart would soar. I felt as if the demons of my past were gone. Micah managed to make it all go away. He made everything perfect.

The door opened, and my head snapped up from the book I'd been staring at while lost in thought to see Micah step into the room. The sight of him made my chest feel lighter.

"Hey, you," I said, trying not to look as completely obsessed as I was.

He looked around, then reached back and locked the door, then smirked at me. "I like the *hot librarian* thing you got going on here. We need to get you some glasses."

I glanced back at the door he'd locked, then at him. "We can't…you know," I whispered, as if anyone could hear us closed off in this room that wasn't much bigger than a closet. Well, maybe a walk-in closet.

Micah walked over to me. "What can't we do, Tink?" he asked as he reached me.

Setting down the book, I stood up from the short little stool I had been sitting on. "Whatever it is you have in mind. Zander has a key to that door. He could come in if he wanted to."

Micah reached out and took one of the loose strands from the makeshift bun I had twisted my hair into earlier and stuck a pencil in it to hold it in place. He wrapped it around his finger slowly. "I've been thinking about how sweet your pussy tastes all day," he said, dropping my hair to cup the side of my face.

I swallowed as my heart rate sped up. "That was just the caramel from the doughnut you smeared between my legs," I replied.

He laughed, lowering his head to mine. "Your pussy doesn't need anything added to it to make it sweet. It already tastes like honey."

Oh God. I was going to have sex in the book return room. How was I supposed to say no to this man when he said stuff like that? Besides, the ache between said legs was now starting to tingle.

His mouth covered mine as his tongue slipped between my lips just as I heard the zipper of his jeans slide down. He picked me up and set me on the edge of the desk, knocking off several books I had in organized piles in the process. Not that I cared.

My skirt had ridden up, but he shoved it up further, and I opened my legs as he stepped between them. His fingers grabbed the crotch of my panties and jerked them aside. With the first thrust, he was inside me, gloriously stretching me to the point of almost pain, but not. Lifting my knees so he could sink deeper, he let out a deep, satisfied groan that vibrated his chest.

"Fuck, I needed this pussy," he said in a deep growl as he looked down at our joined bodies. "You look so damn good, stretched around me like that. Taking my dick like such a good girl, Tink."

My body trembled, and I gripped the edge of the table to keep from falling backward as he pumped into me harder.

"Best fucking cunt I've ever had," he grunted, his eyes taking on a wild look. "I can't get it out of my head. I think about it all the time, Tink. How tight it squeezes me. How amazing you smell. How I want to stay buried inside you, listening to those sexy little cries you make all the fucking time."

He slammed into me, grabbing my waist, and I reached out to hold on to him.

"I want you walking around with my cum dripping out of you all the time. NO one else touches this. MY cunt. My fucking pussy," he snarled as if he were making a claim for someone other than me to hear.

My climax hit me, and Micah covered my cry with his hand as he watched me ride the wave of the orgasm. His eyes locked on mine. I was mesmerized by him. The way his jaw flexed, his eyes flared, and then the slight slack in his jaw as he jerked, then shuddered, pulling me against his chest.

I wrapped my arms around him, gasping as he pumped his release inside me. He hadn't done this before. I had a doctor's appointment tomorrow to start the shot for birth control. He'd gotten tested and then stopped using condoms with me, but he had been pulling out.

I should be worried. We shouldn't be staying here like this. But I didn't want him to let me go. I'd never felt more connected to another person in my life. The part of me that had always felt alone, unwanted, wasn't there. With Micah, I felt complete.

"I'm sorry," he said, pressing a kiss to the top of my head. "I lost control."

"It's okay. I mean, it's safe. Right? I am due to start my period in three days. That's"—I paused, feeling my face flush—"not an, uh, fertile time." Yes, I had Googled it.

"Can't say that has ever been an issue for me. Not something I've had to worry about, seeing as you're the only female I want to shoot my load in like a fucking caveman."

I buried my face against his chest and giggled. Yes, I giggled.

His deep chuckle made me feel warm inside as he held me tighter to him. "You've got my head all kinds of fucked up, Tink."

A knock at the door reminded me where we were, and I dropped my hands and looked up at Micah, panicked. He just grinned like we hadn't just had sex at my job.

"Hey, uh, Dolly. I hate to interrupt, but Professor Yow is here, looking for *Lewin's Essential Genes*. He said you had held it for him," Zander called through the door.

I shoved Micah back and scrambled off the desk, straightening my panties and then pulling down my skirt. "Oh, yes, I'll be right there," I told him.

"Okay." Zander's tone suggested he knew exactly what we had been doing. He seemed to be on the verge of laughter.

I covered my warm cheeks with my palms, scanning the room for the book I had set aside for the professor.

Micah walked over and bent down to pick up a book, then held it out to me. "Looking for this?"

I grabbed it and sighed in relief. "Yes."

He reached out and pulled me to him, kissing my forehead. "Make this quick," he told me. "I'm ready to put you on the back of my bike."

I stared up at him. His bike. He'd had a new battery put in my car, and he had been bringing me to work in my car the past few days. I'd thought he had changed his mind about my riding on his bike. He'd been so against it, as if it were a privilege he wasn't willing to hand out to anyone.

"You brought your bike?" I asked.

"Yeah, Tink." Then, he nodded his head toward the door. "Let's give this to the guy who has a hard-on for me and leave."

I let out a laugh. "You mean, Zander?"

"He's not subtle. Let's just say that."

I patted his chest. "Stop walking around like a sex god, and folks won't drool."

This time, it was Micah who laughed.

Zander was busy helping someone when we left, but he winked at me, then waggled his eyebrows. Micah kept his arm over my shoulders on the way outside to the bike. When we got there, I saw the pink helmet on the seat of the bike.

I paused and looked up at him.

"What?" he asked, trying not to smile. He was pleased with himself.

"You bought me a pink helmet?"

He shrugged. "I assumed that was your favorite color since half the shit you own is pink."

"It is. But that isn't the point, is it, Micah Abe? The point is you BOUGHT me a helmet to ride your bike. You didn't borrow one. You went and picked out one for me."

He smirked then. "You seem real damn pleased about it too."

"It might be the sweetest thing anyone has ever done for me," I admitted.

He picked it up and slipped it on my head, then fastened it like I was a child. When he was satisfied it was on safely, he brushed his knuckles over my chin, but said nothing. I didn't need him to. His actions were far stronger than his words anyway.

I watched as he threw his leg over the bike, then held out a hand for me to take as I climbed on behind him. Once I was settled, he squeezed my thigh, then leaned forward as I wrapped my arms around his middle.

I couldn't think of a time in my life when I had been happier than I was right now.

Twenty-Nine

DOLLY

The parking lot of Paradise Brew, Pepper's bar, was packed. The hurricane had put her back almost a month in opening it. Tonight was her big night. She wasn't thrilled with Micah and me dating, but she'd accepted it. My going to her and pleading with her to talk to her brother had much to do with it. She had finally agreed that I seemed happier and so did Micah.

He had been sleeping at my apartment for a month now. I hadn't been back to the club, but with my work and fall semester starting up, I hadn't had much time. Micah and I had the evenings together. Most weekend nights, he left me after I was asleep to go handle club business, but rarely did I wake up and he wasn't in bed with me.

Tonight, however, was special. We were here to celebrate Pepper's first night with her doors open for business. The number of bikes outside meant that The Judgment had shown up in support. I was so happy for her that I could bust.

Micah bent down and pressed a kiss to my lips before placing his hand on my back and leading me into the bar. A live band was playing, and the place was full. The inside of the bar had a rustic elegance to it. The exposed beams in the ceiling had what looked like antique light bulbs hanging from cords that wrapped around the wood. The bar itself was in the center of the room. It was circular with old barrels lined with mirrors surrounding it. There was dark brown leather seating with occasional black leather mixed in and carved wooden tables that looked as if they'd been made two hundred years ago from the finest oak.

"Stay close to me so I don't have to break a fucker's arm for thinking he can talk to you," Micah said close to my ear as we went farther inside the bar.

This was so far removed from my scene that he didn't have to worry about that, not one bit. He led us to the bar, where Pepper was laughing at some men seated at it, pouring a drink. She seemed to be beaming with excitement. My heart felt full when I saw her like this. She'd been talking about this for years. It had been her dream, and now, she had made it real.

Micah started in the direction of the pool tables, and I noticed Nina at one of the tables beside it, holding a beer in her hand and talking animatedly to Goldie, who was across from her. Nina's husband, Jars, was sitting at the seat beside her with his arm around the back of her chair, leaning back and smiling at whatever his wife was saying.

When we approached them, Jars had already spotted us and pushed out the chair across from him with his booted foot, then nodded for Micah to take it.

"Dolly!" Nina squealed and ran around the table to pull me into a hug.

"She's on the other side of tipsy," Jars said from his seat with an amused smirk.

I returned her hug, smiling, enjoying her enthusiastic welcome.

"I keep telling Micah to bring you back. He's keeping you all to himself," she said, wagging a finger in his face.

"I'll bring her to see you this week," he said with a crooked grin.

"Sit down!" she exclaimed. "We can find another chair somewhere."

"No need," Micah replied, sitting in the chair and pulling me down to sit on his lap. "Keep those legs together. I don't want anyone getting a glimpse of those pink panties," he whispered in my ear.

I felt my cheeks warm, thinking about the fact that he had made sure my pink panties would be damp tonight from his cum before we left.

I crossed my legs and looked up at him through my lashes. "How's that?"

His gaze dropped to my legs. "Fucking distracting."

If he kept looking at me like that, I was gonna have a hard time visiting with his friends.

"Jesus Christ, get a room," Jars muttered.

Nina slapped his arm. "Shut up, you! I'm loving this."

Jars raised his beer and put the bottle to his mouth with a roll of his eyes.

"Micah?" a female voice said.

Before I could even turn to see who it was, I felt his entire body tense up. His hand tightened on my leg for a moment, then released me. I glanced at him, then swung my eyes to whoever had gotten this reaction out of him.

She was blonde. Of course she was. She was also tall and willowy. Long, dark lashes, red lips, and a body that made other women feel inferior.

Please, God, let this be some long-lost relative I don't know about.

"Calista," he replied. His voice was casual, but the way his body was rigid told me something else entirely.

She glanced at me only briefly, and then her eyes swung back to him. "I thought you might be here tonight."

He nodded once. "Pep is my sister," he replied tightly.

"Thought you'd moved to California," Nina said. "You back, visiting your momma?"

She smiled at Nina, and my stomach sank further. She belonged on magazine covers or television. How did she know them? I needed someone to tell me she was related to Micah.

Please, oh please, let that be the case.

"I had some things happen that sent me back home. I've been hoping to run into you actually," she said, and I realized she was looking at Micah, not Nina.

"Yeah, well, you did," he replied.

She was silent for a moment. "I see," she finally said. "It was good seeing you, everyone." Her gaze dropped back to me again. "I'm Calista."

She seemed nice enough. I wanted to think she was nice. I also wanted to think she was a lesbian or a relative of Micah's, but my gut was telling me neither was the case.

"Dolly," I replied.

Calista's catlike green eyes went back to Micah. "She's your…"

"Friend," he replied a touch too sharply.

The relief on her face was obvious. I just hoped the pain in my chest wasn't. He'd called me a friend. Was that what he thought of me? We hadn't labeled what we were doing, but it was definitely not friendly. Not by a long shot.

"I see," she said. "My number is the same," she told him. "I'd love to catch up when you have time."

Micah only nodded once, his jaw clenched tightly.

Calista looked back at the others and said one last good-bye, then turned in her short black dress and strutted on her mile-long legs back into the crowd. Men turned to watch her as she walked by. A few let out whistles. I felt like I was torn between throwing up and bursting into tears.

"She hasn't changed much," Nina said loudly, then held up her hand. "I think this calls for a round of shots. What about some Cuervo?"

Micah's hands were on my waist, and he moved me off him to stand up. "Stay here. I'll be back," he said, not making eye contact with me.

I watched as he walked off and had to force my legs to bend so I could sit down in his vacated seat. He wasn't walking in the direction she had, but why was he acting like this? Who was she? My chest was hurting so bad at the moment that I was struggling to breathe.

"He just needs a minute, sugar," Jars said from across the table.

I looked at him, and I saw the concern in his eyes. They all knew her. Who she was and why Micah was acting so strange. I wanted to ask, but I was scared to know. Terrified actually.

"That boy can't be that stupid!" Nina snapped, glaring after him.

Jars looked at her and shook his head, as if to warn her from saying more. I had to get out of here. I needed some air.

I felt like I was going to suffocate, and if I was about to have a complete breakdown, I'd prefer it not to be where folks could see me. I wanted to do that alone.

A tray of shots was set down on the table in front of me.

"Did I hear someone say y'all needed some tequila?" Pepper asked.

My eyes shot up to meet hers.

"Thank you, Pep!" Nina said, forgetting her moment of anger.

"No problem. You all drink up. I'm taking my girl here for a bit," Pepper informed them.

Pepper held out her hand to me, and I took it, standing up. She pulled me through the crowd, past the bar, and to the door in the back that led to her office. I'd been here a few times, and that was the first room she had finished. Once we were inside with the door shut and the sound of the bar muffled, I walked over and sank into the plush tan chair that sat in the corner.

Wringing my hands together in my lap, I took a deep breath. "Who is she?" I asked, knowing Pepper had seen the woman and that was why she'd come and gotten me.

She let out a heavy sigh. "Calista Churro. Her daddy was in Judgment before he was killed in a motorcycle accident about eight years ago. She only stayed around about six months after that and then left without warning to California. She has an aunt that lives out there or some shit."

I continued to stare at Pepper. There was more. More she was not wanting to tell me. I could see it all over her face. But I also knew she would. Pepper was the most honest person I knew.

She leaned back on the edge of her desk. "Calista and Micah grew up in the club together. They were friends for years until they were more. Micah...well, Micah was in love with her. But Calista could only truly love herself. She'd always been that way, but Micah was too blind to see it. She left him with nothing but a letter, apologizing. I thought he'd chase off after her, but he didn't."

Micah had been in love. Micah had been in love. Micah had been in love.

I felt as if I might break into a million pieces right here. Part of me wished I could.

Micah had been in love. With...a woman who looked like a supermodel.

"Stop it," Pepper said, standing back up and walking over to me. "This was seven years ago. Micah has long since moved on from his childhood love he had for Calista." She bent down in front of me and took my hands in hers. "Don't do this. You're getting in your head and making this more than it is. If he had wanted Calista at any time, he had known where she was and could have gone to find her. He never did."

I took a deep breath, feeling the burn of it all the way into my chest. "He told her I was a friend." My words barely came out as a whisper.

Pepper's hands tightened their grasp on mine. "He's going to regret that. It was just the shock of seeing her here. This thing with you is new to him. He's never in his adult life felt like he does about you with any woman. You make him happy. As much as I was against the two of you, I will admit that I've never seen my brother so damn happy in his life. He's settled. He isn't searching for something. He isn't restless anymore."

"Pepper, don't," I said, shaking my head. "I saw her. I cannot compete with that."

"And you don't have to because you win, hands down. You DO NOT know her. She might look pretty on the outside, but it is skin deep. Micah found that out the hard way. Your beauty is inside and out. *She* can't compete with *you*. She doesn't even hold a candle."

I shook my head just as the door to her office swung open, and Micah came storming inside the room.

His gaze went from Pepper to me. "What the fuck are you telling her, Pep?" he demanded.

Pepper stood up and placed a well-manicured hand on her hip. "What you should have told her before just running off like an asshole."

"I needed a goddamn minute!" he shouted. "I didn't need you to come take her and tell her shit that doesn't concern her."

Pepper threw up her hand and stalked toward Micah. "Doesn't concern her? Are you shitting me right now?!"

"Come on, Tink," he said, looking past her to me. "We're leaving."

I stood slowly, not sure if going with Micah was what I should be doing, but the idea of him leaving me also felt unbearable. He held out a hand in my direction, and like a moth to a flame, I went to it. Knowing that the woman he had loved thought I was a friend of his. She was back and wanted to talk to him. It had affected him too strongly for there to be no feelings left there anymore.

His fingers wrapped around my hand, and he tugged me closer to him. "Congratulations on your opening," he said to Pepper, then all but dragged me toward the door.

"Don't fuck up," Pepper warned him.

He didn't turn around or even slow down. We walked through the bar and right back to the front door we had entered earlier. I didn't look around or make eye contact with anyone, although I knew every Judgment in here was watching me being hauled away by Micah.

When we got outside and I saw my pink helmet sitting on his bike, I wanted to burst into tears. I had thought his buying that meant something. That it had been his way of saying I was his. That we were together. That he cared.

He didn't say a word as he walked me over to his bike, put my helmet on me, as he always did, then climbed onto the bike. I took his hand and threw my leg over, sliding in close to his back, then wrapped my arms around him.

Tears burned my eyes as I inhaled the leather vest and wondered if this would be my last time on the back of his bike.

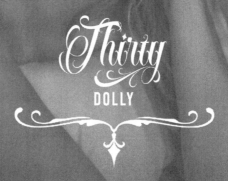

Thirty

DOLLY

walked into the apartment after Micah unlocked the door and opened it, then stepped back for me to enter. Silence. He hadn't spoken one word to me, and I wasn't sure what to say. Everything I'd thought I knew had been snatched away from me in moments. The security I had started to feel with him was gone.

"What did Pepper tell you about Calista?" he asked me.

I turned around to see him standing there with his arms over his chest defensively. As if I had something to answer for and this was all my fault. I wanted to scream at him. Hit him. Make him hurt the way I was, but I knew I'd never do that.

"That you grew up together. You were in love with her, and she left after her father was killed," I said simply.

He swore under his breath. "Did she tell you I was eighteen years old? That it's been almost seven fucking years?"

I nodded.

"Then, why do you look like that?" he asked, staring at me.

"Like what?" I asked, my voice barely above a whisper.

He dropped his hands to his sides, then tilted his head, and his expression softened. "Like I hurt you. Like I did something wrong and you can't stand to look at me."

I frowned. "What Pepper told me wouldn't have had a punch if you hadn't introduced me as a friend, then left me without any explanation." I let out a hard laugh, then found that my pain was starting to turn to anger. "I guess I should have clarified exactly what it was we were doing here. I seem to have gotten my wires crossed what with you staying with me every night, fucking me, buying me a freaking pink helmet!"

Micah's brows drew together, and he took a step toward me. "Did you just say fucking, Dolly Dixon?"

I scowled up at him. He wasn't going to change the subject. Not now. Not when he had just pierced my chest like he had.

"Don't," I warned him, taking a step back.

"Don't what? You don't want me near you now? Because some girl from my past showed up and I didn't respond the way I should have?"

I shook my head, narrowing my eyes at his beautiful face. "No. I'm just trying to decide if I want to keep *fucking my friend* or not," I spat out, surprising myself.

He moved fast, and before I could move, his hands grabbed both my arms and held me still. I tried jerking free but realized it was pointless, so I just glared up at him.

"If the word *fucking* comes out of that pretty mouth one more time, I will turn you around and fuck you right here over this sofa. Now, if you want to talk about tonight and Calista, then we will do it. Yes, I handled it wrong. She had surprised me. Seeing her pissed me off. Her walking up to me like she had every right to made me fucking furious. But I shouldn't have called you a friend." He paused, then sighed. "I don't really know what to label us, Tink. I've not thought about it. I just wanted her to leave."

Girlfriend would have been an easy word to think of, but I didn't say it. I bit my tongue because I wanted him to keep talking.

"She is my past. My youth. She means nothing to me."

"You loved her," I said.

He sighed, then nodded. "Yeah, I did."

The little repair his words had done to my shattered chest was undone with those three words. I swallowed against the lump in my throat. It was closing in, getting tighter.

One hundred twenty-two, one hundred twenty-two, one hundred twenty-two.

"But it was a long time ago. Whatever love there was has been gone for years," he said, then brushed over my lips with his thumb. "The woman I want to go to bed with tonight. The one I want in my arms. The one who makes me forget all this shit and the one I want to sink my dick into is you. Just you, Tink."

But he didn't love me. He wasn't ready to call me his girlfriend.

This was something though. We had just been together or doing whatever it was we had been doing for a month now. I couldn't expect him to fall in love with me so fast. But...I stared up into his face and knew I'd do whatever he asked of me and deal with the pain. Because I loved him.

The words *not enough* were back, hammering in my head. Trying to take the happiness I had found with Micah away. Reminding me of my flaws. The people who hadn't wanted me. Who hadn't fought for me.

"Tink?" Micah's voice called out to me.

I blinked, then focused on him again.

"There you are. Where did you go?" He brushed his knuckles along my cheek. "Come take a shower with me. I'll wash your hair."

I nodded, fearing that this was the beginning of the worst heartbreak I'd ever experience. Calista wasn't going to disappear. She wasn't going to be less beautiful, and she wasn't going to forget Micah. I knew that. It all came down to, did I trust him? Or was that even something that I should be considering? If he realized he still loved her, it wouldn't be a matter of trust. It would be a matter of the heart. Just like I couldn't stop loving him…if he loved her, how could I expect him to just stop?

One hundred twenty-two, one hundred twenty-two, one hundred twenty-two.

I stood, looking out the window in the kitchen as I drank my espresso.

Last night, Micah had been sweet and attentive. He'd made me come six times before we finally both passed out from exhaustion. Twice, I had done that squirting thing that he loved so much. I was still unsure how it happened because it wasn't me controlling it. The stronger the orgasm, the more likely I would do it. That much I had figured out.

I heard Micah's footsteps only moments before I felt his hands come around me. Smiling into my cup, I leaned back against him and sighed. He'd told me over and over last night how special I was and how much he wanted me. It hadn't been a declaration of love, but it had soothed my fears some. Enough that I could breathe deeply again.

He bent down until he could nibble on my ear. "I woke up hard, and you weren't there," he said in a raspy, sleepy voice.

I laughed and looked back at him, tilting my head so I could see his eyes. "You always wake up hard."

"With the smell of you on the sheets, reminding how good that pussy is, I can't help it."

Shaking my head, I laughed again and turned back to my espresso.

Micah reached around and took it from me. "Pull up this flimsy nightie and bend over the table," he ordered me before swatting my butt with his hand.

I started to ask for my espresso back when his hungry gaze met mine. His eyes roamed over my pearl satin nightgown, as if he wanted to rip it off my body. That was enough to change my mind and do as I had been told. I walked over to the table and bunched the nightgown around my waist, then leaned forward, placing my palms flat against the wood.

"Goddamn, that's a pretty ass," he growled as I looked over my shoulder to see him shove his boxer briefs down before grabbing my hips and angling them up. "Spread your legs, baby."

Going up on my tiptoes, I opened them wider and inhaled deeply as he slid inside of me.

"Fuuuck yes," he moaned. "That's so good. I love seeing my good girl bent over, being bad for me. I tell you to do it, and you do it. Drives me insane."

His hips began to piston in and out of me. The table shook beneath me, and I cried out every time he sank deeper.

"That's my cunt," he said with his next thrust. "Always wet for my cock."

Strangled sounds came from me as his dirty words and praise sent sparks of pleasure through me. I wanted to make him feel this way. I loved knowing I could. Lifting my bottom more for him, I was startled when his palm landed hard on my left butt cheek.

"Leaving me in bed alone," he said harshly. "Makes me want to see this round ass red from my hand."

"Oh God," I moaned as my head fell forward.

"You like that, baby? You like me spanking your sweet ass?" he asked as his hand slapped the other side.

"MICAH!" I screamed as my sex pulsed, and the promise of my coming orgasm began to build inside me.

He slapped my bottom harder this time, then cursed. "Fuck, I love the way it jiggles."

I closed my eyes tightly, unsure if that was praise or not.

"Take my dick, baby," he panted. "Hot little pussy."

The wave hit me, and I clawed at the wood as I let out screams of pleasure. The rush from between my legs made my legs tremble as I felt my body convulse.

"FUUUCK! That's it. Squirt all over my cock, baby. FUUUCK!" His fingers bit into my flesh as he began to jerk behind me. "GAH!" he shouted as he pulsed inside me. Filling me up. Marking me.

I rested my forehead on the table, panting as his hold on me eased, and he slowly pulled out of me.

He ran his palms over my bottom and squeezed gently. "You drive me crazy, Tink."

It wasn't love. But it was something.

Thirty-One

DOLLY

I finished wiping down a table at Paradise Brew and headed for the kitchen.

After her opening weekend, Pepper had underestimated how busy she would be during the week and called me today after I got home from my classes to see if I could come in and help. Micah hadn't taken me or picked me up today. He had club stuff to handle, and Liam had called him to Ocala this morning for something going on there.

Happy to help my friend and not have to go home alone, I dropped off my books, stopped by to take Jeremy leftovers from last night that he could heat up, then headed to the bar. Pepper handed me a pair of black shorts and a cropped red T-shirt that had *A drink in Paradise* on the front and Paradise Brew's logo on the back. Once I had changed, she had given me a quick rundown of things and introduced me to her staff.

So far, things had been going smoothly. Several of The Judgment guys came in, and I took their tables. A few college kids were at the pool tables, and some men that worked at a local power plant were at the bar. We stayed busy enough that there had been no time for her to ask me about Micah and what had happened on Friday night. I knew he hadn't spoken to her since then, but I had texted with her a few times, assuring her that things were fine.

Momma, on the other hand, had surprised me by stopping by yesterday, and Micah's laundry that I had washed was still folded on the coffee table. That hadn't gone over well. She had the church prayer chain praying for my soul, and I expected a visit from the reverend any day now. Wouldn't that be a sight if he came by when Micah was there?

"Hey, Dolly," Tex greeted me as he sat down at the bar just as I walked back out of the kitchen to bring out some fresh lime wedges.

"Hey, you," I replied.

"Pep got you working, huh?" His eyes traveled down my body, and a crooked grin tugged at his mouth. "Micah seen you in that outfit yet?"

I shook my head. "He's in Ocala. This was a last-minute thing. Pepper's been busier than she thought she'd be, and I needed something to do anyway."

Tex nodded. "I sure hope I'm here when he gets a look at it. Might stick around longer than I planned in case he shows up."

"Stop stirring the pot," Pepper scolded him and slid a beverage napkin across the bar in his direction. "Miller draft?" she asked.

He nodded, then cut his eyes back to me. "Heard about what happened with Calista. You doing okay?"

I nodded. "Sure. Just fine," I replied, wanting to get away from him before he asked me any more questions I didn't want to answer. Talking about Calista was something I'd rather not do.

The sound of chair legs scraping the floor caught my attention, and I turned to see Grinder moving away from the table he'd been at toward the entrance.

"What the fuck are they doing in here?" Tex asked, standing up from his stool and following Grinder.

"Shit," Pepper muttered, throwing down her bar towel and hurrying around the bar to go toward the entrance.

Two men had just walked in the door, and one of them I recognized. Bolt was a member of the Crowns MC. He'd been nice to me, but then that had been when I was with Canyon. I hadn't known him really. Just like I hadn't really known Canyon.

"Tex! Grinder! Step back. This is my bar, and I can serve who I want to serve," Pepper called out before the two of them made it to the Crowns members.

"You gonna serve that Acree piece of shit if he walks in here too?" Grinder asked her, looking pissed.

Pepper put a hand on her hip. "No, but if he does, I'll handle it. These two I haven't got a problem with, so go on back to your drinks and let them be." She swung her gaze back to them. "You two here to cause a problem?" she demanded.

Bolt held up his hands and shook his head. "No, ma'am. We came for a drink. We can leave if need be."

She waved a hand at the empty tables. "Have a seat. Tonight's menu is seafood gumbo or shrimp and grits," she told them, then turned to shoot a warning glare at Tex and Grinder before making her way back to the bar.

When she got back to the bar, she looked at me. "You got a problem waiting on them, or do I need to go see if Jimmy can leave the kitchen to come do it?"

"I can do it," I replied.

"Damn, your balls," Tex said to me before taking a drink of his beer.

"It's fine," I assured him and took my pad and pen out of my apron, then headed to their table.

Bolt glanced up at me as I approached and smiled. "Didn't expect to see you here, Dolly."

I shrugged. "Can't say I was expecting you to walk through that door either," I replied, making him chuckle.

"Fair enough," he said.

"What can I get y'all?" I asked him before he started up small talk. That I wasn't gonna do.

He was still Canyon's friend, and I hadn't heard anything from Canyon in a month. Micah had said he'd given The Judgment the one hundred grand he owed them and that I'd have no more problems with him.

"I'll take a Corona with a bowl of that gumbo," Bolt told me, then looked over at the other man.

He seemed nervous as his eyes darted around the room. I wasn't real sure that was a good sign.

"Same," he replied, finally looking up at me.

I didn't need to write that down to remember it so I told them I'd get the order in and be right back with their drinks before leaving the table. Heading back to the bar, I put the food order into the computer system, then went to grab their beers.

"You know either one of them, Dolly?" Tex asked me.

I nodded. "Bolt. He's the one with the shaved head," I whispered.

As I was turning to leave, I saw Tex on his phone. It was obvious he was texting someone. I just hoped he wasn't stirring up trouble.

When I placed the beers in front of the men, Bolt looked up at me. "How ya been, Dolly?" he asked.

"Good, thanks. And you?" I replied, trying to be polite.

"All right. Finally got patched in," he said with a crooked grin.

From listening to biker talk since being with Micah, I knew that meant he wasn't a prospect anymore. He was a real member of the Crowns. Ringer was a prospect with The Judgment, and he'd explained it to me one day on the way to work.

"Congratulations," I told him, knowing it was a big deal.

He nodded. "Thanks, Dolly. Miss seeing you around."

I wasn't sure what to say to that, and before I could think of anything, the door to the bar opened, and I glanced over to see Micah striding inside with Country behind him. His eyes locked on me, barely giving the men at the table a glance. I could tell from here that he was angry.

"Order should be ready soon," I told the men and made my way toward Micah.

His heated gaze took in my outfit, and I watched his jaw clench tighter. When he reached me, he grabbed the back of my head and bent down to crush his mouth against mine. This wasn't what I'd been expecting, and like every time Micah kissed me, I melted against him, seeking more of it.

The kiss was demanding and almost painful. I grabbed on to his vest for balance just as he eased up, and then he gently bit my bottom lip before releasing me.

"You need to change," he said to me, his expression still as fierce as it had been when he walked in.

"This is the uniform Pepper gave me," I explained.

He grabbed my chin. "Don't care, Tink. Go change."

Seeing as how I had missed him today, which was a given, I didn't want to argue right now. He had surprised me by coming back early. I was thrilled about that, but he was embarrassing me in front of the entire bar.

"I don't see what the problem is," I replied.

His hand gripped my waist tightly. "Go fucking change."

"Is everything all right, Dolly?" Bolt asked.

The rage lit up Micah's eyes immediately, and it had me grabbing his arm with both my hands.

"I'll change. Come with me," I urged, then glanced at Bolt. "We're just fine," I told him with a bright smile.

Micah took a step toward the men, and I held on to him with all my body weight.

"Let's go, Micah."

The fury in his expression as he glared at Bolt had me ready to call for Pepper. She had to be back in the kitchen, or she'd have been over here, handling this.

"You don't fucking speak to Dolly. Don't breathe in her direction," Micah snarled.

Bolt smirked. "She's our waitress. Might be difficult."

"Not anymore," Micah snapped and threw his arm over my shoulders, then began walking us toward the back. His entire body was strung tight.

I didn't say anything until we were inside Pepper's office with the door closed. But once we no longer had an audience, I spun around and stared up at him.

"Micah, why are you so worked up? Is it that Pepper let Crowns in the door or the fact that I'm wearing what all her waitresses wear?"

"Both," he clipped out. "I can see entirely too much of your skin, and those bastards don't get to talk to you like they fucking know you. Get on some goddamn clothes!"

I stepped closer to him and placed my hands on his chest. "I won't go near their table again. I'll have Pepper do it. But this is the uniform. Pepper is even wearing it."

"I don't give a fuck what Pepper is wearing. But I don't want other men seeing what's mine."

What's his? I stood there, staring up at him, trying not to smile like a lunatic. He'd just called me his. Yes, I was his, but hearing him say it when we weren't having sex and he wasn't talking about my vagina made my heart squeeze.

"Okay," I said finally. "I'll change."

He narrowed his eyes, studying me. "You will?"

I nodded.

"Thank you."

"On one condition," I told him.

"What's that?"

"When we go back out that door, you don't cause any problems for Pepper."

He scowled. "She shouldn't have let the fucking Crowns in here."

"They're paying customers, and this isn't a bar owned by The Judgment."

He sighed and nodded. "Fine. But you stay away from their table. If that bastard tries to talk to you again, I'll put his head through the fucking wall."

I smiled then. "Noted. Now, go back out there so I can get changed."

Micah ran his hand over my bare stomach. "I want to watch."

"No."

"Why?"

"Because Pepper needs my help, and if you watch me change, then…"

"I'll bend you over her desk and fuck you. Is that what you're saying, Tink?"

I nodded, feeling my face flush as my body instantly began to tingle.

"Looks to me like you want to be fucked, baby. That needy look just clouded those pretty eyes," he said, taking a step toward me.

The door swung open, and Pepper came storming in, looking almost identical to Micah when he'd walked in the bar tonight and seen me waiting on the Crowns.

"I have three new tables out there, Micah! Stop causing problems and making a scene!" she yelled at him.

He held up both his hands. "I'm not causing any problems. I just want Tink in some clothing that covers her up more."

If looks could kill, Micah would be dead.

Pepper stalked over to him and jabbed his chest with her pointer finger. "That's real fucking rich, coming from a man who used to date strippers!"

Micah grabbed her wrist. "Fuck. Not date. And they weren't Tink. You know it's different." He dropped her wrist then and looked back at me.

Some of Pepper's anger eased, and her shoulders rose and fell with a heavy sigh. "FINE! Let her wear her own clothes. But please don't say another word to the Crowns. They're eating their food now, and since six more Judgment have walked in the door, I doubt they are going to stick around long."

Micah smirked. "I expect several more will arrive before they're done eating."

Pepper rolled her eyes. "Figures. They'd just better all order lots of drinks and food."

Micah nodded. "They will."

She pointed to the door. "Get out so she can change."

Micah frowned. "I hate to be the one to break it to you, Pep, but I've seen her naked."

Pepper held up a hand to stop him. "Don't. I know that. I also know the moment I walk out of here and she starts to undress, you'll fuck her in my office. One"—she held up a finger—"that's not an image I like to dwell on." She held up a second finger. "And two, I need her out there, waiting on tables. Now, get out."

Micah grabbed my chin and tilted my head back before pressing a kiss to my mouth, then turned and walked out the door.

Pepper looked at me and shook her head in exasperation before following him.

Thirty-Two

DOLLY

Thanks for last night. I needed that more than you know.

*T*hose words kept replaying in my head. I could even hear them said in *her* sultry voice.

I stared at the cup of espresso I had made, but the thought of actually drinking it made me feel nauseous. Setting it on the bar, I walked out of the kitchen. The world that had been so bright and full of hope just an hour ago when Micah woke me up, kissing down my body, now felt as if it had no oxygen left in it. Everything that made me smile had been snatched away so quickly.

The sound of the shower cut off, and I stared toward the bathroom door. Micah was in there. After we'd had sex, he'd kissed me and held me, then said he needed to get a shower. He had to head back to Ocala today but would be back late tonight. We had been in a bubble of perfection—or so I'd thought. Instead, it was my own delusional bubble. One I had created in my mind.

I wasn't sure how I could face him now. Did I confront him? Ask him what the text from Calista meant? Maybe there was a good explanation that I needed to hear, and then this devastation that I was experiencing would go away. I'd have my bubble back. The one that I shouldn't have started to feel secure in.

Micah hadn't said he loved me. He hadn't called me his girlfriend or labeled what we were. He basically lived here now. We were together every chance we got. Sex was amazing. The thought that he was seeing Calista…it felt almost unreal.

The faucet turned off, and I knew he was finished brushing his teeth. He would open the door and walk out at any minute now. His towel would be wrapped around his waist. All of his beautiful body on display. It was one of my favorite morning views.

Except now, all I could think was, had Calista seen it too? What had they done last night? What was it she had needed that he had supplied?

My stomach rolled, and I closed my eyes and inhaled deeply through my nose. Even if Micah didn't love me, he cared. He'd called me his. He wouldn't betray me that way. Would he? Could he do that? The man I loved didn't have that kind of cruelty in him.

The door to the bathroom opened, and the moment he saw me, he smiled that slow, sexy grin that usually made my heart flutter. This morning, it didn't flutter. It cracked.

Asking him was the only fair thing to do. For me and him. I was going to dwell on it, and this would just get worse if I didn't know.

"You already had your espresso?" he asked me.

I couldn't smile. I didn't even try. I shook my head. "No."

He studied me for a moment, and a frown creased his brow. "What's wrong, Tink?"

Knowing the truth was better than making up my version of it, I had to hold on to the hope that there was a reasonable explanation.

Dropping my gaze to the floor, I took a deep breath before asking, "Where were you last night?"

He didn't respond right away. Dread, fear, loss—it all began to uncurl inside my chest. Why wasn't he saying anything?

"I told you, I was at the club. We had some issues to handle."

I swallowed hard. He was evading the answer. I could hear it in his voice. There was more, and he didn't want to tell me. Too bad. His phone had lit up when I was getting out of bed, and the text had been right there on the screen for me to see.

"Calista texted you." I lifted my eyes back to look at his face. I needed to see it. If he was lying, I'd be able to tell.

His nostrils flared. "You reading my texts now, Tink?" he asked with accusation in his tone.

I thought I'd have preferred he slap me across the face. It would have been less painful.

"Not exactly. I was getting up, and you got a text. I glanced down and saw it. Not on purpose, but then I hadn't thought you had anything to hide."

He narrowed his eyes. "I don't," he replied. "But it seems like you've already made your assumptions."

I shook my head. "No. That's why I am asking you what it was about."

Micah let out a hard laugh. "I don't answer to anyone. You can either trust me or not."

I refused to cry in front of him. He wasn't giving me anything here, and it sounded like he wasn't going to.

"I trust you. But I don't see why I can't ask what you were doing with Calista last night."

"That isn't your business. Don't make this something it isn't, Dolly."

Dolly. Not Tink. To think, once, I had hated the name Tink. Hearing him say my name now was like an insult. As if I had been knocked down on the ladder of importance to him. Did he have a nickname for Calista? Had he called her by it last night?

"I see," I managed to get out past the agony gripping me by the throat.

He shook his head. "Whatever. I can't deal with this shit right now," he said, sounding annoyed before walking into the bedroom.

Unable to move, I stood there, battling on what to do now. Did I apologize? Or did I go in there and demand he tell me? This was my business. We were…together. Right? It felt like we were. He had called me his. That made us a couple. Didn't it?

I flinched at the sound of him slamming a drawer shut. He was angry. Why did he get to be angry? It was me who should be slamming drawers. Not him. Nothing had been done to him. I hadn't caused him to question me. I had been here last night. In my bed. Sleeping. Trusting him.

He walked back out of the bedroom, shrugging on his vest over a black T-shirt I had washed yesterday for him. When he got to the door, he grabbed his keys from the table and paused before turning his gaze to me. "I'll see you tonight," he said simply.

Nothing more.

I nodded, and then he opened the door and left. It was the first time he'd done that without kissing me in a month. Since we had become whatever it was we were.

My vision blurred as the tears filled my eyes, then began to slide down my face. This wasn't how it was supposed to be. Loving someone shouldn't be like this.

I stared at the door, waiting, praying it would open back up and he'd walk back inside. The rev of his motorcycle was faint, but I heard it in the silence of the apartment. He was really leaving me like this.

Loving someone enough for both of you wasn't easy. It seemed I was about to find out just how hard it could be.

Turning my head toward the kitchen, I let my thoughts go to the paring knife. The relief that would come from that would be instant but fleeting. The shame would come shortly after. It always did.

This time, I had to fight it. I couldn't rely on someone else to be strong for me. I had to find that strength inside myself. When it all was stripped away, it was me I was left with, and that girl I had been was grown up now. I could overcome the past. It was time to conquer my demons.

The library was busy today, and that helped keep me from getting inside my own head. I focused on each task at hand and didn't try and work through what had happened this morning. When I had first gotten to work, I had almost texted Micah that I was sorry—twice—but I'd turned my phone off and put it in the back office so I wouldn't be tempted to pull it out in a moment of weakness.

I had nothing to apologize for. He did. I loved the man, but I needed to love myself too. Not cutting this morning had been a milestone for me. In the past, that would have sent me down a spiral. It made me feel stronger, walking out of the apartment this morning without hurting myself. It had been a small step, but it was giving me the will to take more.

"Do you mind running this book over to Professor Nobleman?" Zander asked as he held out a thick textbook to me. "I would, but there are five more books I need to pull for other inquiries."

I took the book. "I got it," I assured him. "Any other books I need to deliver?"

He shook his head. "Not at the moment."

The art building was half a mile away, but with the traffic and parking, it would be faster to walk it over there. Heading out the door and down the steps, I realized too soon that walking alone was going to give me time to think about Micah. I tried to think about the essay I had to write for my psychology class and the dynamic with my mom as the point of interest. She'd never read it, so I should be safe from getting my earful.

The sun was extra bright, and I squinted as I stopped at the crosswalk. I wished I'd grabbed my sunglasses. This was sure to give me a headache. My eyes were sensitive. At least the pain of a migraine would dull everything else. Like the constant, heavy ache in my chest that Micah had left there.

"Dolly?" A female voice called out my name.

I turned to see Calista walking from the library parking lot in my direction. She was wearing a pair of skintight jeans, a sleeveless red blouse, and high-heeled black boots. Her long blonde hair was blowing in the breeze, and I hated that she reminded me of a shampoo commercial.

Why was she here? Had Micah sent her to explain things to me?

I held on to that hope tightly as I waited for her to reach me.

"Can I help you?" I asked her when she stopped in front of me with that perfect white smile of hers.

"Yes, I came to talk to you. Do you have a minute?"

"I'm taking this book to a professor, but I can spare a few seconds," I replied, unable to keep the dislike from my tone.

"I shouldn't have bothered you at work. It's just that Micah told me you saw my text, and I feel terrible about you thinking it meant something it didn't. He said for me not to worry about it, but I can't help it. You seem awfully sweet, and"— she paused and gave me a small, apologetic smile—"Micah is…well, Micah. He doesn't think about women's feelings. I've been dealing with some things, and Micah listened to me last night. He's always known me better than anyone else, and we…we've always had a connection. Time and distance haven't changed that. He was able to help me with things and clear my head. Nothing more happened."

Every word that came out of her mouth felt like the paring knife in my kitchen was slicing away at my skin all on its own. I stood there, listening to the only woman Micah had loved tell me they had a connection and he'd helped her with things last night. Listened to her. Been with her. Even if they hadn't physically done anything, he'd emotionally been with her. In a way he never had with me.

"I see," I replied because any other words would be too hard to verbalize.

"I still love him. I always will," she told me. "And to be fair, I want you to know that's why I came back."

What little hope I had left, the strands I had been clinging to, all snapped free at that moment. I stood there, staring up at the woman who could take Micah from me. Who would take Micah from me. I would be left with nothing but memories of a one-sided love affair, and he'd forget me.

I just nodded. No words would come.

What would I say even if they did? I couldn't claim him and fight back. You couldn't fight for something you never had.

She, on the other hand, could. She'd had everything I wanted, and she was back to take it.

She slid her sunglasses down over her eyes. "I just wanted to clear the air. I know you're important to Pepper, and I don't want her upset with me. I thought at least smoothing things over with you would aid in that."

Still, I said nothing.

"I'll let you get back to work," she replied, then turned and walked away.

I stood there, watching her go. Not moving. Unaware of the world around me. I had to snap out of it. I knew I did.

Turning, I stepped out onto the road as the anguish of all I had almost had and already lost sank in. The honk of the horn and the sound of screeching tires barely registered in my head. Physical pain radiated through my entire body, and then the blackness rushed over me. I clung to it, thankful for blessed relief.

Thirty-Three

MICAH

"Ohe's working with Acree. The tracker you slipped on her last night confirms it," Liam said, walking into his office that sat above the strip club in Gainesville, Florida, that The Judgment had bought three years ago so he could be close to his daughter and grandson.

"Fucking bitch," I muttered, not surprised.

Calista showing up had been a red flag. Liam agreed with me, and we'd decided the best thing to do was track her. See where she was going and who she was with when she wasn't trying to get me alone to talk to her.

"He's got bigger balls than I thought, or he's the stupidest fucker I've ever known," Liam said, handing me the printout of Calista's locations since I'd planted the tracking device on her last night.

She'd left River Styx, where I had agreed to meet her at midnight, and gone straight to the Crowns' compound. She'd been there all night.

"I saw how messed up he was when Gage was done with him. He's physically scarred for life. There has to be some fucking screw loose in his head. Challenging us is challenging them. And he got a taste of what the family will do to him. Is one hundred grand really worth it, or do you think he's seeking revenge and thinking he can use Calista?"

Liam shook his head. "No fucking clue. But you need to make sure that everyone is on alert. Use Calista to your benefit. Get info out of her if you can and see if you can get a recorder on something of hers. Any communication she has is important."

I shook my head, thinking about this morning with Dolly. That had been fucking brutal. "I can't pretend with Calista. Dolly saw a text from her this morning, and she's not happy about it. I was caught off guard and fucking pissed Calista had texted me. I didn't know what to tell Dolly, but I gotta get back and fix shit."

Liam raised his eyebrows and leaned forward on the desk, resting on his elbows. "You're worried about hurting Dolly?"

I nodded.

A grin spread across his face, and then he let out a bark of laughter. "I'll be goddamn."

I wasn't amused. "Don't," I snapped. "This is about finding out what the fuck Canyon is up to and stopping it. I want Calista out of town. Away from me and The Judgment."

"Because her being around is upsetting Dolly?"

"No. Yes, but you know it's more than that. It's the fucking scum that I don't trust."

Liam nodded and leaned back in his chair, still grinning at me like I was a damn sideshow.

My phone rang, and I glanced down at it and saw Tex's name. He knew what we were dealing with today, and I had him keeping an eye on Calista while I was gone. I didn't trust her not to go after Dolly. She saw her as competition, and Calista didn't like it when she felt as if she had to compete. What she didn't realize was, Tink wasn't competition.

She was mine.

"Yeah," I said, answering the phone.

"You need to get back," Tex said, his voice tense.

"What's wrong?" I asked, standing up, my eyes locked on Liam's.

"It's Dolly, man."

My heart slammed against my chest as I gripped the phone tighter. "What's wrong with Dolly?" I demanded, finding it hard to suck in air.

"She was hit. By a car. She's at the hospital now. I'm here. Just get here," he said.

"What the fuck?!" I roared.

Nothing could have prepared me for the terror that shook me.

"She walked in front of a car." He paused and let out a heavy sigh. "You need to get here."

No. No. No. This wasn't happening. I couldn't lose her. No.

"What hospital?" I asked hoarsely.

"Mercy."

"Tell her I'm on my way."

He didn't say anything, and I felt as if someone had shoved their hand into my chest and yanked out my fucking heart.

"I will. If she wakes up."

I ended the call, my eyes burning as well as my lungs as I struggled to breathe. This wasn't happening. It couldn't be happening. Not my Tink. I couldn't lose her.

"FUCK!" I roared as I grabbed the chair I was in and hurled it across the room.

"Micah, what's wrong?" Liam asked, coming around the table toward me.

"I have to go. It's Dolly," I choked out.

"I'll drive. You can't drive like this."

"The fuck I can't!" I snarled and stormed out the office door, then broke into a run down the stairs and out into the parking lot.

Slamming through the doors the nurse had pointed me to, I paused as my eyes scanned the packed room. Pepper shot up out of her chair in the midst of Judgment members, prospects, and ol' ladies. Her face was stricken, eyes swollen and red, and I felt like my world had just been snatched from me.

"Where is she?" I asked her.

"Surgery," she replied. "They think there is internal bleeding."

"FUCK!" I shouted, my voice laced with the agony gripping me. I bent down with my hands on my knees as the pain seared through my body. "What happened?" My voice was thick and hoarse. It didn't even sound like me.

"You need to sit down," Pepper told me. "Come with me." Her hand touched my back, and I flinched.

"I can't sit down, Pep. I can't fucking breathe."

I heard her sniffle, and I gripped my knees tighter.

"Don't cry. Don't you fucking cry. She's going to be okay. She has to be okay. She has to. She has to be okay."

I heard her small sob, and I jerked away from her. I couldn't listen to her cry. It meant she doubted that Tink would make it.

"Tell me what the fuck happened!" I demanded to no one in particular. I just needed an answer.

"Calista went and talked to her. I followed her, watched it," Tex said from across the room.

The look on his face almost doubled me over again. I needed someone to tell me she was going to be okay. Not look as if they were preparing for a damn funeral.

"I don't know what she said, but it upset Dolly. I was waiting until Calista left to go check on Dolly, but she turned and walked right into oncoming traffic."

Calista. Fucking Calista. I was going to kill her and Canyon Acree too. Both of them would die.

"I called 911 as I ran to check on her. I was with her the entire time. Until they put her in the ambulance. Then, I followed it here," Tex explained.

I saw the blood on his shirt beneath his vest now. Dolly's blood.

"Mrs. Dixon," Pepper said, snapping my attention from Tex to the woman walking into the room.

She was petite, older, had darker hair than Dolly's, but the mouth and eyes were the same.

"What happened, Pepper?" the woman asked, her eyes damp with tears and her nose bright red as she clenched a tissue in her hand.

"She didn't see a car and stepped out onto the crosswalk, Mrs. Dixon. They have her back in surgery now," Pepper said, putting her arm around the woman.

I watched as Dolly's mother looked around the room and tensed up, her eyes widening.

"It's okay," Pepper assured her. "These are friends of Dolly. They care about her. That's my brother, Micah."

Mrs. Dixon's eyes swung over to look at me. She assessed me slowly, then sniffled and wiped at her nose again. "I guess that explains a lot," she said, then narrowed her eyes at me. "Dolly is a good girl. She was raised to do right."

I nodded my head. "Yes, ma'am."

She sighed and let out a small sob. "Last I talked to her, I was upset. We had words."

Pepper kept her arm around the woman. "She knows you love her. Girls argue with their moms."

"But she's fragile, and it's my fault," the woman said as a louder cry came from her.

Pepper walked her over to the chair she had been sitting in, and Grinder jumped up out of the seat beside it so that Pepper could sit down with her. I saw Pep whispering to her and consoling her.

Looking at her, I wanted to feel sympathy. But I couldn't. I agreed with her. She had let Tink down. She'd allowed her to suffer abuse I still didn't know the details of. I wasn't sure I could forgive the woman for that. Tink had deserved more as a child. She'd needed protection, and her mother had failed her. It was a momma's job to protect their children. Tink had no one.

The image of her bloody thigh and the knife on the kitchen table felt like its own raw blade ripping at my soul. Dolly had been through so much. She'd survived. She had been strong and overcome more than anyone should have to. Now, she was in there, fighting for her life, and the last thing I'd said to her was cruel. I hadn't reassured her like she needed. I hadn't told her what she had been asking with those amber eyes of hers.

I had been too fucking scared to say it. She needed to hear it, and I hadn't been able to say it. The realization that I might never get the chance destroyed me.

I leaned back against the wall and stared at the door, willing a doctor to walk through and tell me she was going to be okay. That I could go see her.

"Liam just texted," Jars said to me.

I looked in his direction.

"He and Hughes took some men and are headed to find Canyon now. He said to tell you to stay here. Keep him updated, and they'll handle the rest."

I wanted to be the one to face Canyon. I wanted it to be me who tortured him, but I wasn't leaving Tink.

"Tell him to hold Acree until I can deal with him."

Thirty-Four

MICAH

The doors opened after what felt like a fucking eternity, and a doctor walked inside the room.

He paused for a moment, then cleared his throat. "Is the immediate family of Dolly Dixon present?"

I didn't wait for her mother to speak before walking across the room to the man who looked barely old enough to be out of college. "How is she?" I demanded.

He blinked and took a step back as he stared up at me. "And you are immediate family?" he asked, his tone giving away his nervousness.

"Yes," I barked. "How is she?"

He cleared his throat and looked around the room.

"I'm her mother," Mrs. Dixon said, stepping up beside me. "Is my daughter going to be okay?"

The doctor glanced back at me, then turned his gaze back to Mrs. Dixon. If he didn't start talking, I was going to pin him to the goddamn wall with my hand around his throat.

"The most serious injury is the punctured lung," he said, shifting his attention to me only briefly. "We have her sedated, and the chest tube has been put in place. The good news is, there is no brain bleed, which had been a major concern since her head was hit and the amount of blood she lost. The fracture to her tibia is an open one. Meaning it broke through the skin and surgery was required to set it." The doctor smiled at Mrs. Dixon. "It was touch and go for a minute, but Dolly is going to be fine. She came through everything perfectly. You should be able to go back and see her in the next couple of hours. A nurse will come get you." He paused and took in the room of bikers again, then looked at me. "It will be limited visitation at first with just immediate family."

"I understand," Mrs. Dixon replied, then let out a sob. "Thank you. Thank you so much."

The doctor nodded, then turned and got out of the room as quickly as he could.

Mrs. Dixon turned to Pepper and threw her arms around her neck. "She's gonna be okay. Thank you, Lord!"

Pepper patted her back and looked at me as she held Dolly's mother. Her eyes were damp with tears of pure relief.

I leaned back against the nearest wall and closed my eyes. Dolly was okay. She had some bad fucking injuries, but she would heal. I'd take care of her. She'd be fine.

I sucked in a deep breath and hung my head. I could have lost her. The best thing that had ever happened to me, and I'd almost lost her.

"You okay?" Pepper asked, and I lifted my head to see my sister standing in front of me. Her eyes glistening with unshed tears.

"I am now," I said hoarsely.

She let out a shaky sigh. "Yeah, me too."

I rested my head back on the wall. "I love her, Pep."

She smirked. "I know. I just wasn't sure you did."

"I've known. I should have told her already."

Pepper reached out and squeezed my hand. "Yeah, you should have. But lucky for us, you get to tell her now."

I nodded. "We fought this morning. Or rather, she questioned me about a text that Calista had sent, and I didn't handle it right. I should have told her the truth. Trusted her with it. I'm just not used to sharing things. I'd never had to before. And Calista went and said something to her. Upset her." I closed my eyes. "Fuck, Pep. She was hurt. Because of me."

Pepper squeezed my hand again. "Then, you fix it. Dolly will listen. She's the most forgiving person on the planet. She also loves you. I didn't need her to tell me that either. The way you two look at each other is a like a damn billboard. The obnoxious light-up kind that you can see miles away."

A smile tugged at my mouth for the first time all day. Well, except when Dolly had woken up this morning and cried out when I ran my tongue between her pussy lips. That memory had my grin spreading. Her surprised little expression before she moaned my name had been perfect.

Tex walked up to us and put his hand on my shoulder. "Your girl is gonna be fine. And Liam called. They have Canyon, but Calista is gone. She dumped her phone and purse outside of the city limits. Headed north on 95, it looks like. Canyon will talk, and they'll know how to find her soon. Keets also called Liam. He wasn't aware of Canyon's actions. He's taking his patch for it and asked that the Crowns not be held accountable for Canyon. That he acted alone."

Wolf Keets was the president of the Crowns MC. He didn't seem like the kind that would be clueless as to what his VP had been doing, but this was Liam's call. I had to focus on Tink. Getting her better. Other than killing Canyon, I didn't want to deal with the rest of it right now.

I just nodded. "Fine. Whatever the board thinks. I just want Canyon."

"Yeah, he knows."

I didn't want to be away from the waiting room, but Liam had called twice, so I'd stepped outside the hospital to see what he wanted. Besides, I needed a minute away from Mrs. Dixon and her disapproving scowls. The woman was never going to like me.

"Canyon started talking as soon as he found out Dolly was hurt. Not sure everything he's saying is true, but he's being cooperative. How's Dolly?" Liam said when he answered my call.

"Still waiting on them to tell us we can see her, but she's going to be okay." I wasn't going to be okay until I saw her, talked to her, told her all the shit I should have this morning.

"Canyon said Calista came to him. She wanted Dolly out of the picture, and she did some digging and found out about them and told him if he'd help her get Dolly away from you, she'd handle you herself. Canyon said he told her he didn't want to get messed up with The Judgment anymore. Seems he did fuck her a few times, and she stayed over at the Crowns of her own choice. Not his. And when Canyon found out about Dolly being hit by the car, he lost it. Went to shouting that he was gonna slice Calista's throat open and watch the bitch bleed himself. Either the man missed his calling in the theater, or he's got it bad for Dolly. I don't think he had anything to do with what happened at the library. The kid who hit her had no connection. He was looking down at his phone, and when he looked up, it was too late. At least, that's his story. We haven't questioned him. I think the only thing Canyon is guilty of is fucking Calista and being in love with Dolly."

My hand fisted at my side, and I fought the urge to find a cigarette. The fucker wasn't getting near Dolly. She was mine.

"You against me killing him for thinking he loves what's mine?" I asked.

Liam chuckled. "Go take care of Dolly. Forget about Canyon. He's not a threat. When we find Calista, we will let you know."

"She pays for this. Someone has to," I told him.

"I know," Liam replied before ending the call.

Thirty-Five

DOLLY

I blinked against the bright light several times, then closed my eyes again.

"Dolly? Honey, it's Momma. I'm here."

I heard my mother's familiar voice and then felt her smooth, cold palm cover my hand.

"Is it too bright? Here, I'll turn off the lights," she said, and her touch was gone. "There," she said. "That should be better."

I opened my eyes again and stared up at her, hovering over me.

"Thank you, Jesus," she breathed, grabbing my hand in hers. "You scared me good."

I tried to talk, but my throat felt too dry.

"Are you in pain? I can call the nurse."

I raised my hand to touch my throat. "Water," I whispered.

"Right! Let me go get a nurse. Don't try and move. They closed up your chest after they took the tube out, and your leg is in a cast."

The horn, the impact of the car, and...Tex's voice. I remembered seeing his face. He had begged me to stay with him. That Micah needed me. I winced at the thought. Micah. Closing my eyes again, I wished I hadn't woken up. The darkness that had pulled me under had been pain-free. Not just the physical, but the emotional too.

"The nurse is coming, honey," Momma assured me. "You did real well in your surgeries. You're gonna be right as rain again before we know it. The church is getting meals lined up for us, and Mary Margaret and Sue Ellen are already at the house, getting your bedroom fixed up. The prayer chain has been hard at work. Everyone is praying. You're gonna be just peachy keen." She patted my arm.

She had just described hell to me. Funny how all the church folks' good work was a level of hell I did not wish to visit. But then, did I have another choice? I didn't know all my injuries, but from the way I felt, it wasn't good. She had said my leg was messed up, and it didn't feel like I was going to be getting up to walk anytime soon.

"Pep," I choked out.

I needed Pepper. She'd save me from going back to Momma's. I didn't want to burden her, but she could help me come up with a better option.

"Oh, she's in the waiting room. Has been since even before I got here. They said only one at a time could be back here for now. You want me to send her back?"

I nodded.

"And the nurse is here. She can get you comfortable. Pepper will be here in just a sec," she assured me, then thankfully left the room.

A lady with short auburn hair and bright green glasses stepped up to the bed. "I'm going to sit you up enough to drink some water, but I need you to sip it slow through the straw. I got you a cup of ice, too, that I'm going to leave beside your bed. You can let that melt in your mouth, and it'll ease the raw throat from where the breathing tube was. How is your pain level on a scale of one to ten—one being barely nothing to ten being excruciating?"

"Six," I replied barely above a whisper.

"I'll add some morphine to the IV and see if we can get it down to a four at least. Sip slow," she said as she placed the straw between my lips.

"Dolly," Pepper said, and I finished taking my sip to look over the cup at her.

I smiled at her, thankful that she was here. If I'd only had my momma here for this, I might have forced myself to slip into a coma just to escape. Pepper would help buffer Momma and all her good intentions.

The nurse moved back, and Pepper rushed to my side and grabbed my hand in both of hers.

"You scared the shit out of me. I've never been so terrified in my life," she said, reaching up and brushing some hair off my forehead. "You're not allowed to cross a street alone again. Do you understand me?"

"I'm sorry," I said, feeling guilty for what I must have put her through. I couldn't imagine how I would feel if the situation had been reversed.

"Don't apologize. You can make it up to me later. I can't stay in here long. Micah is about to rip the entire hospital apart with his bare hands if he doesn't get in here to you. He's already threatened the lives of two nurses and a doctor."

My eyes widened. "Micah?" I asked.

"Yeah, you know, the asshole brother of mine who can't stay away from you? Remember him?"

The memory of Calista and what all she had said before I was hit replayed in my head.

"I don't want to see him," I said. "I can't, Pep."

She sighed heavily and tilted her head to the side. Understanding in her eyes was clear, but I knew her well enough to know that she was about to try and talk me into seeing him.

"Dolly, he needs to explain some things. He's been real messed up about this. I've never seen him this pitiful. Not even when our dad died. Just listen to him, okay? Trust me?"

"I just can't," I croaked. "He feels guilty, and I can't listen to him. See him. I need time."

Pepper leaned down closer to me. "Yes. He is blaming himself, but that is not what he wants to say. I swear, you need to just listen to him."

"No." I couldn't do it. I wasn't in the right state of mind. Healing from one thing at a time was all I could handle.

"Dolly—"

"No!" I said firmly. "No!"

Pepper finally nodded. "Okay. Calm down. I'll talk to him. Maybe he won't destroy the waiting room and kill any employees who stand in his way."

I already knew he wasn't going to fight that hard to get back here to me. He would probably be thankful for the reprieve. It would give him more time before he told me he was still in love with Calista. That he cared about me, but we were over.

"I'm sure it'll be fine," I said.

Pepper didn't look convinced. "Do you want me to send your momma back? I'd come back, but someone is going to have to control Micah. I'm the only one he might not punch."

I rolled my eyes. "Momma can come back, but don't leave me with her long. Please. She's trying to take me to her house when I'm let out."

Pepper raised her eyebrows. "Oh, I can promise you right now, that won't happen."

I wanted to reach out and hug her. "Thank you."

She smiled. "Not me you need to thank, but nevertheless, I'll go deal with the beast outside and send your momma back. If I can. I'm not making any promises. But I will do my damn best." She turned and left the room without explaining herself.

I tried to reach the cup of ice, but moving hurt too much. Taking deep breaths was painful as well. In fact, just about everything was throbbing or aching in some way.

Loud voices caught my attention outside the door, and I listened, but it was muffled. There was some shouting, and the door swung open. Micah entered the room, looking... rough. His eyes were wild, his hair looked like he'd run his fingers through it and pulled it in different directions, and he was breathing hard.

"I tried!" Pepper called out as Micah closed the door, not taking his eyes off me.

He took long, determined strides toward me. When he reached me, he grabbed the edge of the bed, and his head fell forward as he let out a weary sigh.

"Fucking hell, Tink. You took years off my life, baby." His hand slid under mine, and he held it. "There aren't words to tell you how sorry I am."

"Don't," I said, wincing from an agony worse than the injuries to my body. "I can't. I know. You're forgiven. Just go, Micah. Please."

His blue eyes searched my face, and I realized they were bloodshot.

"No. I'm not going anywhere. There's a real good chance I'll never leave your side again. I can't go through something like this again."

I stared up at him, not real sure what he was saying. Guilt was one thing, but this seemed like more.

"Calista came to see me," I told him.

He nodded, and a darkness settled over his expression. "I know. She'll pay for it too. I won't rest until she suffers a hell worse than what she did to you and what I was put through today."

His hand tightened over mine, and he pulled the chair my mother had been sitting in up as close as it would get to the bed, then sat in it so he was eye level with me.

"She loves you," I told him.

If he was going to force me to do this now, then I needed to rip myself wide open and get it done.

"No, Tink. She loves herself. She always has. But even if she did love me, it wouldn't mean shit." He leaned forward, his eyes locked on mine. "Because I'm so goddamn in love with you that I can't see anyone else. I just see you. Everywhere I go, you're all I think about. When shit gets bad, I want you because I know that when I see you, my world will be set right again. You're my own little sunshine that I don't deserve and I sure as shit never expected. But from the moment you looked at me across that bar with those gorgeous eyes, I wanted you. I just didn't know then that I'd come to need you. You're mine, Tink, but I'm yours. I can't be anyone else's. You own me."

He reached over and brushed a tear from my cheek with his thumb. "Now, tell me you love me. I need to hear it. Today has threatened to take my damn soul. Love me, Tink."

I sniffled. "I do."

A small smile tugged at his lips. "I need to hear the words, baby. Give me that. Please."

I turned my hand over in his and squeezed it back. "I love you, Micah Abe."

Thirty-Six

DOLLY

"Your momma hates me," Micah said, walking into his room at the club, carrying a tray of food.

I sat up in bed and tried to hide my wince from the pain. I'd told him I didn't need to take my pain medicine this morning. I hated the way it made me groggy.

"She'll grow to love you," I replied. "Did she call again?"

He nodded, setting the tray down. I could see Nina's homemade bread and Goldie's cheese grits, along with several other things. "She isn't a fan of you being here. I think her exact words were, 'You're keeping her in the devil's lair, and the Lord can't heal her darkened soul if you don't free her from the sinfulness in those walls.' "

A laugh bubbled out of me as he got the lap tray and set it over my legs.

He grinned. "You think that's funny, huh?"

I nodded. "Sorry. I wish Pepper hadn't given her your number."

He pressed a kiss to my mouth, then stood up. "I'll get her back."

I had no doubt he would. "Well, if you could, don't do it today. She said she was bringing me some more of my things."

Micah put a plate of food on the lap tray. "What do you need? I thought you had everything?"

I looked down at his T-shirt I was wearing. "My night-gowns and panties, for starters."

"What's wrong with my shirts? And why do you need panties?"

I smiled up at him. "I just want to feel like me, and I need panties because...well, I just do."

He sat down on the side of the bed and slid his hand under the covers to caress my good leg. "You can't feel like you in my shirts?"

I shrugged.

"If you have on panties, it makes it harder to do this," he said, slipping his hand between my thighs. "I like having the easy access to my pussy when I want it."

Inhaling sharply, I laid my head back against the headboard.

"See, you like it too," he pointed out, pulling my leg open, then thrusting his finger inside of me.

I grabbed at his arm and moaned.

"You want me to move this food and put my face down there? Make you feel even better?" He leaned in and nipped at my earlobe. "I like you here, in my bed, wearing my clothes, with this sweet little cunt bare for me."

Trembling, I grabbed at the sheet with my other hand and lifted my hips, which hurt my chest and leg, causing me to cry out.

Micah stopped. "You're hurting."

"It's okay. I shouldn't have moved that way."

His hand was gone from between my legs immediately, and I watched as he stood up, sticking his finger in his mouth and sucking it as he walked over to my meds sitting on his dresser.

"Fuck, you taste good," he said, then picked up the pain pills before turning back to me, still licking the finger he'd had inside of me like a lollipop. "Now, be a good girl for me and take your medicine. If you do, I'll lick your pussy until you beg me to stop."

"You drive a hard bargain," I replied. "But if I wanted your mouth between my legs, all I'd have to do is ask real nice."

He smirked. "You think so?"

I nodded. "Yep."

He chuckled and narrowed his eyes at me. "Fine. That's true, but don't use your power against me. Take the pain meds, Tink. I can't stand the thought of you hurting." The pleading look in his eyes was the only reason I was going to give in.

"I'll take them, but they make me sleepy. I don't want to sleep."

"What if I get in bed and hold you while you sleep?"

I sighed. "You have things to do."

He shook his head. "Nothing more important than you."

"Micah."

"Tink."

We stared at each other for a moment, and then he winked.

"Come on and play nice. Take the meds. Eat your lunch, and then I'll eat your pussy. After, we can snuggle."

"Well, when you put it that way," I replied.

"That's my girl."

Yes, I was in fact his girl. Completely.

And Micah Abe was also mine.

Acknowledgments

Another year. Another insane publishing schedule. Without these people it wouldn't be possible.

Britt is always the first I mention because without him, I wouldn't get any sleep, and I doubt I could finish a book.

Emerson, for dealing with the fact that I must write some days and she can't have my full attention. I'll admit, there were several times she did not understand, and I might have told my seven-year-old "You're not making it in my acknowledgments this time!" to which she did not care. Although she does believe she is famous after attending some signings with me. But that is not my fault. I blame the readers ;)

My older children, who live in other states, were great about me not being able to answer their calls most of the time and waiting until I could get back to them. They still love me and understand this part of Mom's world. I will admit, I answer Austin's calls more now because he happens to have my first grandbaby on FaceTime when he calls.

My editor, Jovana Shirley at Unforeseen Editing, for always working with my crazy schedules and making my stories the best they can be. This summer she has gone above and beyond with this crazy schedule of mine and this fall it doesn't slow down. She's a rock star.

My formatter, Melissa Stevens at The Illustrated Author. She makes my books beautiful inside. Her work is hands down the best formatting I've ever had in my books. I am always excited to see what she does with each one. Each book seems to be better than the last! It's amazing.

Autumn Gantz, at Wordsmith Publicity, for saving me from losing my mind and taking over all the things that I can't keep up with anymore. Her help allows me to write more. Send her cookies.

Beta readers, who come through every time: Jerilyn Martinez, and Vicci Kaighan. I love y'all!

Sarah Sentz, Enchanting Romance Designs, for my book cover. I am in love with the way it looks.

Abbi's Army, for being my support and cheering me on. I love y'all!

My readers, for allowing me to write books. Without you, this wouldn't be possible.

Printed in Great Britain
by Amazon